The Stiff in the Study

Viola Roberts Cozy Mysteries:
Book 2

Shéa MacLeod

Dedication

To my aunts, Becky and Charline, who are always up for shenanigans.

Shéa MacLeod

Acknowledgements

So many people have helped with Viola's second story that it's hard to thank them all properly, but here goes.

To Alin Barnum for coming up with one of Viola's more hilarious exploits

.

To Dan J for the vehicle expertise.

To B for the brainstorming sessions.

And to the wonderful people of the city of Astoria, Oregon, who welcomed this crazy writer on her researching journey, particularly the women who give their time and attention to the glorious Flavel House Museum. I learned so much.

.

Shéa MacLeod

Chapter 1

I'd have given anything for a really juicy murder.

A romance novelist's life involved skirting one unmitigated disaster to another. Or maybe that was just me. The current disaster was a raging case of writer's block, so bad that dead bodies were starting to sound good. Even relocating from my writing den at home to a table at my favorite wine bar wasn't helping. Maybe I should give up historical romance and write crime thrillers?

I sighed and glanced around Sip. It was a cozy place with a wide front window overlooking the Columbia River, warm red walls, and wide plank floors. Racks of wines—all from Pacific Northwest wineries— lined nearly every wall and a great deal of floor space. The rest of the room was taken up by little round tables covered in cheerful red and gold cloth so patrons could sit and enjoy a glass. Or bottle.

Nina Driver, who not only owned Sip but was a good friend of mine, was busy behind the bar unpacking boxes of newly delivered cabernet. Her long, honey hair tumbled about her shoulders as she hummed softly to the old-school jazz playing over the stereo system.

At the end of the bar sat one of the more colorful denizens of Astoria, Oregon. A regular at Sip, Lloyd was somewhere between sixty and eighty, his craggy features and wild beetle brows making it impossible to tell which.

His white hair stood straight up as if he hadn't brushed it in days, maybe a week even. He leaned heavily on the bar, staring soulfully into a glass of red.

I scowled at my laptop screen, willing words to appear. No luck. I had a looming deadline, and the story was stuck.

"You lied to me, Scarlet," he said, his manly chest heaving. (Did manly chests heave? I'd have to look into that.) "I can never forgive you."

"But Rolf," she cried, "I did it for your own good." Tears poured down her beautiful face, turning her blue eyes a stormy gray.

Good grief, that was melodramatic. My readers would love it. But what did Scarlet lie about? That was the million-dollar question. And if I couldn't answer it, I'd be the next dead body, thanks to my editor.

"I could kill him!" Portia Wren stormed into Sip and slammed her turquoise designer purse on top of the polished wood bar, hard enough to make a substantial thwack. She hiked herself onto one of the tall stools. Her snug blue and green dress slid up her thighs like it was trying to escape the laws of gravity. She didn't seem to notice, but Lloyd sure did. His eyeballs nearly popped out of his head, despite him being three sheets to the wind already.

"Keep your eyeballs in your head, Lloyd." The order was snapped out from behind a rack of Bordeaux where Nina was stocking up. I would swear the woman had eyes in the back of her head.

Portia and I shot Lloyd a scowl, though he couldn't see me since I was sitting behind him. He dove back into his wine glass with gusto. It wasn't that anyone could blame Lloyd, exactly. Portia had a way of attracting attention. The woman had curves that wouldn't quit and dressed like a runway model, despite Astoria being a small, wet, coastal town and not Milan or Paris.

"You look like you could use this," Nina said, emerging from behind the rack. She was a tall woman, though not as tall as Portia, and her voluptuous figure was crammed into a cranberry knit dress. She set off the ensemble with knee-high, black boots and her naturally pouty lips painted with a cranberry-color lipstick. She may have passed the fifty mark, but I could only aspire to be half as sexy as Nina.

She set a large wine glass in front of Portia and held up a bottle. I knew without looking that it would be a dry, oaky chardonnay—the only kind Portia ever drank. The minute the glass was full, she snatched it and chugged back half in one go.

I used the interruption as an excuse to escape my laptop. I got up and joined Portia at the bar. "Who do you want to kill? And can I help?" I asked, only half kidding. Mess with my friends, feel my wrath. I may not look scary, being of the short and plump variety, but believe me, I'm devious.

Portia snorted delicately. "The Louse."

"Oh," Nina and I chimed in unison.

"The Louse" was August Nixon, Portia's boss at the local museum, Flavel House. The gorgeous landmark

3

Victorian that drew tourists from around the globe was, unfortunately, run by a big, fat jerk.

"Better be careful about making murder threats," Nina joked. "Viola will have to hunt you down and see that justice is served."

I rolled my eyes. One time. One time, I—Viola Roberts, author of bodice-ripping Western romances—solved a murder and now it was an eternal joke among my friends. "More likely I'd help her hide the body. What happened, Portia?"

She sighed and swallowed her remaining wine before handing the glass back to Nina for a refill. "I was in one of the storage rooms doing inventory, and he cornered me. Started putting his gross, sweaty hands in places he shouldn't." Her face was nearly as red as the walls of Sip, making her short, platinum hair look like a nimbus of white fire.

"You need to report that...jerk," Nina said. Clearly, she'd wanted to use a stronger word, but Nina didn't like to swear at work. Outside of work, she swore like a longshoreman. "No wait, forget that." Nina waved off the idea of reporting Nixon. "Knee the sucker. Right in the—"

"I think reporting him is the better option," I interrupted. While kneeing her boss in the delicates would probably be satisfying, Portia would likely be the one who ended up in trouble, in this day and age. "Turn him in. Report him for sexual harassment. This is not okay."

"You think I don't know that?" Portia scowled. "But who am I going to turn him in to? He's the boss. And it's not like we have an HR department. I am the HR department."

She had a point. Astoria was a small town, and the museum had just four employees, two of which were part-timers. There were another half dozen volunteers who showed tourists around on weekends and during the summer months. Basically, August Nixon was king of his Victorian castle.

"How about the head of the historical society?" I suggested. "Surely they have some say in the matter."

"Please. The Louse is loaded. And he's got all kinds of powerful friends, including the mayor and a judge. No way they're going to kick him out. Not as long as he wants the job."

I grimaced. That was the problem with this world. Those in high places got away with murder, sometimes literally, while the rest of us paid for it. But I didn't want to focus on the negative. I needed to help my friend.

"You could report him to the police," I suggested. "That won't look too good for him with his fancy friends. Might knock him down a rung or two."

"Yeah, and he'll make my life even more miserable," Portia groaned, taking another deep swallow of wine from her glass, which had been magically refilled. Every move was elegant. I caught Lloyd peeking at her again and threw him another scowl.

I stared out the large front window. It had been a rare sunny spring day, and the early evening light glinted off the water below. It was nearing sunset. Magic time.

The bell above the door jangled as a group of tourists walked in. Nina excused herself to greet them and hand out the daily wine list. Sip was one of those places where you could buy a bottle (or case) of wine, and sit at the bar and drink it. Or just have a glass. It was also the local watering hole of sorts for those who preferred wine over beer and conversation over ear-bleeding music or giant TV screens full of sports. It was also about the best place to catch up on town gossip, which was why I liked it.

"So," said Portia, changing the subject, "have you heard from Lucas lately?"

I felt myself blushing and told myself sternly not to be an idiot. "Oh, you know, now and then," I said, trying to play it cool. I fooled no one, certainly not Portia.

I'd met Lucas Salvatore several months earlier at a writer's convention in Florida. The same convention where I'd found a dead body, been accused of murder, and managed to get both myself and my best friend Cheryl Delaney into and out of trouble. Like Cheryl, Lucas was a thriller and mystery writer. He also had a secret love of romance novels. Go figure. Although we'd been on a few dates, it was difficult, what with him living nearly two hours away in Portland.

Portia and I chatted over wine as the sun sank into the bay and our stomachs began to rumble. Lloyd had long since staggered off, and the tourists had departed to the nearest eateries. Only a couple die-hard locals were left.

Portia and I waved goodbye to Nina and headed out into the cool evening. "I'm meeting Cheryl for dinner. You want to join us?" I asked Portia as I shrugged into a lightweight jacket and twisted my long, dark brown hair up into a quick bun to avoid wind tangles. Clouds were beginning to scuttle across the darkened sky. No doubt there would be rain before morning.

Portia shivered. She hadn't brought a jacket, silly girl. "I'll take a rain check. Right now all I want to do is get my pajamas on and curl up with some mind-numbing TV."

We said our goodbyes, and Portia sashayed away, nearly giving a passing tourist a heart attack. He did a double take so hard he nearly tripped over his feet. His wife angrily smacked him on the back of his head and stormed off. He stumbled after her making loud protestations of his innocence. I hid a smirk as I turned to walk uphill toward Fort George Pub.

Astoria is built on a hill where the Columbia River meets Youngs Bay before flowing out to join the Pacific Ocean. The docks are on the waterfront, naturally, with the town center running parallel to the river a couple blocks in. From there, the city marches uphill toward the Astoria Column, the crowning glory of Coxcomb Hill. I'd read once that the monument was patterned after the Trajan Column in Rome. I've never seen it— the one in Rome, I mean—so I couldn't tell you if that's true.

Most of the houses in Astoria were glorious old Victorians painted in wildly bright colors. Made the town look like a mini San Francisco. But sprinkled in between were Craftsman cottages, a few Cape Cods, and the odd modern home.

Fort George Pub was in a renovated warehouse a block up the hill from the main drag. I made it in record time to find Cheryl already there, sitting at one of the rustic tables, a pint of something golden in front of her. Personally, I hated beer, but Cheryl enjoyed the odd glass. She waved me over with a grin.

She was dressed similarly to me in jeans, boots, and a casual top. On me, it looked relaxed and comfy. On her, it looked stylish and charming. Her short, brown hair stood up in cute little spikes that would have made anyone else look like they'd just rolled out of bed. On her, it was artistic and stylish.

"So, how goes the writing?" she asked as I took the chair across from her.

I rolled my eyes. "Same as ever."

She gave me a look of sympathy. Only another writer could understand the frustration of writer's block. "Really? Getting out of the house didn't help?"

"Not even a little. Maybe I need a trip to Eastern Oregon or something. See some real cowboys. Visit a ghost town. I don't know."

She gave me a look. "You don't even like cowboys."

I shrugged. "Anything for my readers." It was true. I didn't much like cowboys, ranches, country music, or any of that other stuff that one might think went along with writing historical Western romances.

"Speaking of...how is the gorgeous Lucas?"

"Were we speaking of that?"

She glared at me. "What is your problem, Viola? You've got a gorgeous, smart, talented, not to mention rich guy who is totally into you, and you act like you're about to visit a dentist's office."

She was right. It was nuts. I should be throwing myself at the man, but that wasn't my style. Plus, I'd gotten used to being alone. Other than a brief flirtation with marriage in my early twenties, I'd avoided long-term commitment. It wasn't for me. Although Lucas Salvatore seemed to be shaking that long-held belief. Still, I wasn't ready to go there.

"How about you?" I said, switching the subject. "Meet anyone interesting lately?"

"Men," Cheryl said with a scowl. "I've got no time for them. I've got a deadline, you know. This book isn't going to write itself."

"I hear you."

The waiter interrupted with our burgers, and we both dived in. Mine had bacon jam and bleu cheese. The smoky bacon and tangy cheese was absolutely perfect, and I nearly moaned in delight.

I felt badly for Cheryl. She'd met a lovely man at the Florida conference. It had seemed like things were going well, despite the differences between them—he lived on the East Coast and she on the West. He was a vegetarian; she wasn't. That sort of thing. Then he dumped her to get back together with his old girlfriend. It had taken a lot of Ben & Jerry's to get her over that one. She was still pretty much off men, even though I kept pushing. Gently, of course. It was my job as her best friend.

While we ate, I told her about Portia's troubles with The Louse as well as our conversation about dealing with the situation. "She seems to think she's stuck. That there's nothing she can do."

Cheryl snorted. "Maybe she should go with Nina's first suggestion. Consequences be hanged."

"Believe me, I'm tempted to do it for her."

We were waiting for the waiter to bring us our check when my phone started playing "Everybody Have Fun Tonight" by Wang Chung. I literally had no idea how my ringtone had gotten changed. Probably one of my nephews. They were always doing things like that as pranks when I visited my sister in Portland. I probably should have changed it back, but I liked the catchy tune. The caller ID told me it was Portia.

"Hey, girl," I shouted cheerfully over the din of the pub. Maybe she'd changed her mind. "We're at Fort George. Want to join us?"

"Viola, I'm at the museum. You've got to come quick." She sounded panicked, which wasn't like Portia.

"Is everything all right?" I asked, digging around in my purse for bills. I threw some on the table, not caring if I was overpaying or not.

"No, everything's not all right," she wailed. "The Louse has been murdered!"

☐

Chapter 2

I was grateful the Flavel House had a burgundy carpet in the study. It made it harder to see the blood. And there was blood. Quite a bit of it. Some of it had splattered on the books lining the shelves and on the antique fire screen near the body. I winced inwardly. The body. I felt sort of badly for calling him "The Louse" now, but not too badly. The man had been a menace.

August Nixon was sprawled on the carpet, sort of crumpled like a rag doll in front of the grand fireplace. He'd been a pudgy man, balding and pale from too much time indoors and not enough sun outdoors. Typical Pacific Northwesterner. He was wearing a sweater vest in an unfortunate shade of beige. I could see dark stains around the collar. My stomach turned.

Next to the body lay a heavy, brass statuette of Eros. There was a sticky residue on one corner along with a few strands of hair. Obviously the murder weapon. I remembered seeing it gracing a hall table near the front door. Talk about abuse of artifact. The historical society would have kittens. It was obviously a weapon of opportunity. Did that mean the murderer hadn't come here to kill Nixon? That it had been a spur of the moment thing? Maybe a crime of passion? Or perhaps the murder was planned, but the killer knew he'd have plenty of choices. No sense risking getting caught with a gun in your pocket.

"What happened?" I asked Portia, who was hovering in the doorway, purse still clutched frantically to her chest. Her usually alabaster skin had gone pasty white. She should probably be sitting down, but that might mess with the crime scene or something, so I shoved her out into the hallway and urged her down onto a red velvet loveseat.

"Ah, well, I headed home, like I told you, and as I passed the museum, I saw a light on." Portia lived about three blocks up the hill from the museum in an ultra-modern condo building. It looked totally out of place in Astoria, but fitted her personality to a tee. "I figured I'd better check, just in case somebody forgot to turn off a light. But when I got here..." She shrugged as if what happened next should be obvious.

"You called the police?"

"Of course. Right before I called you." I could see her hands shaking where she clutched her purse straps.

Fort George was only a few blocks from the museum. It had taken me about five minutes to walk it, which explained why I'd gotten there ahead of the cops. Something I doubted they'd be thrilled about.

"Did you touch anything?" It wouldn't be good if her fingerprints were all over the crime scene. Though, of course, she worked there, so it wouldn't be that odd.

"Of course not," she snapped, voice going shrill. "It was obvious he was dead, and I've seen CSI."

I heard voices out on the front porch. The police, no doubt. I quickly poked my head back into the study and glanced around the rest of the room. Besides the bookshelves, there were two large, comfortable-looking chairs with a table between them. On the table, a lamp glowed softly, and next to the lamp was a prosecco bottle and two empty glasses, one of them with a lipstick smear on the lip. Magenta, it looked like. I glanced at Portia. Her lipstick was a bright vintage red. I'd never seen her wear anything else. Besides which, Portia never drank anything but chardonnay. A woman had definitely been here, and I couldn't imagine it had been long ago. There was still condensation on the bottle.

I slipped my phone out of my pocket and snapped a picture of the lipstick for future reference. Just in case.

The fact that Nixon would use the room and its priceless furnishings for some sort of assignation was repugnant. He was supposed to be protecting the historical building and its collections, not using them for his own ends. I guess they didn't call him the Louse for nothing.

The tromp of masculine feet in the hallway jarred me out of my thoughts. It wouldn't do to let the cops catch me hovering around the body. I darted back to join Portia on the loveseat and wrapped my arm around her waist, just in time for the police to arrive.

The first man was middle aged and dressed in a neat charcoal-gray suit with a plain white, perfectly pressed shirt and a blue and yellow striped tie. His black dress shoes were shined to high gloss. I recognized him immediately: James "Bat" Battersea. Although I'd grown up in Portland, I knew very well he was a big deal in Astoria. He was a hometown boy and had been a baseball star back in high school (hence the nickname "Bat"). Everybody thought he hung the moon and stars. He was a decent sort of fellow and did a lot of good things for the community, but I'd never run across him in a crime-solving capacity, so I had no idea of his experience with homicide.

The other two were uniformed officers, both male. Were there no women on the Astoria force? Seriously, this was the twenty-first century.

"Are you the ones that found the body?" Bat asked in a brusque, no-nonsense tone. The sort of tone that informed everyone that he was in charge and wouldn't put up with any shenanigans. Well, tough. I was the Queen of Shenanigans.

Portia hesitantly raised a hand. "I did."

He turned gimlet eye on me. "And you, ma'am?"

I tried not to glare. I hated when people addressed me as "ma'am." I wasn't that old. "Portia called me after she rang the police. I'm here for moral support."

He gave an exasperated sigh and turned to the younger of the two police officers. "Chambers, take these two ladies outside and wait for me."

The cop nodded eagerly and waved us down the hall. Portia was all too eager to comply. After a parting glance through the open doorway at the crime scene, I followed reluctantly behind.

Chambers led us out the front door and onto the wide, wraparound porch that hugged the massive Victorian. There wasn't anywhere to sit, so I made myself comfortable on the top step. It was a little chilly, but not too bad. The porch had a good view of the town below as well as the lights of the ships hovering off the coast.

Portia sunk down next to me and opened her mouth like she meant to say something, but I shook my head slightly. Chambers might look like an innocent, young newbie with his big hazel eyes and freckled nose, but I'd bet my last crumpled dollar that he was prepared to report anything we said to his boss. I reached over and squeezed her hand, which seemed to calm her slightly.

At some point, the medical examiner arrived. Or what passed for one in Astoria. In actuality it was Mr. Voss, the local mortuary owner and funeral director over at Slumber Rest. He'd store the body until the state medical examiner could collect it and do a proper autopsy in Portland. Voss crept up the stairs like the shadow of death while his assistant wheeled a gurney up the walkway. One wheel squeaked loudly in the silent evening. They should see about fixing that. It was distracting.

It felt like hours before Bat's footsteps echoed down the hall. He appeared in the front doorway looking as neat and orderly as he had before. His expression was a mask, giving nothing away. He'd have made an excellent poker player.

He made his way down the steps so he could stand in front of us. He stared at us for a full minute. If he thought either one of us would break, he had another think coming.

"Now, Miss—" He turned to Portia, one eyebrow lifted, waiting.

She swallowed. "Wren. Portia Wren."

"You said you found the body? When was that?"

"A little past eight. It was just getting dark."

"Bit late to be working."

She fidgeted, twisting her fingers in her lap. "I wasn't."

"She'd been down at Sip with us all evening," I barged in. Last thing we needed was the detective focusing on the wrong person.

"And who is 'us'?" he asked.

"Nina Driver and me. Nina owns Sip—"

"I'm familiar with Ms. Driver," he cut me off rather rudely. "So, you left work for the bar at what time?"

"Um, a little after five." Portia's voice was squeaky with nerves. I squeezed her hand again.

"She arrived at Sip at precisely fifteen minutes past," I injected.

Bat gave me a look of annoyance. "And you know this how?"

"I was on my computer at the time. I happened to look at the clock when she came in, of course."

He looked like he'd sucked on a lemon. "Of course." He turned back to Portia. "And you left Sip when?"

"Eight. Or maybe a little after."

"Eight-oh-five," I interrupted again.

"Ms. Roberts." Ah, so he did know who I was. "Would you please refrain from interrupting?"

"Just trying to help," I said, leaning back against the step and crossing my arms. He ignored my glare.

"Why did you come back to the museum after hours, Ms. Wren?"

"I passed by on my way home. I happened to see there was a light on in the study, which there shouldn't have been. I figured I'd better check it out."

"Why not call the police?"

She gave him a confused look. "Why would I? It wasn't like there was a break-in. I figured somebody accidentally left the lamp on. It happens."

"Was anyone here when you entered the building?"

She shook her head. "Not that I could tell, but I saw the light was on in the study. I went to turn it off." She looked a little faint. "And that's when I found him."

The questions went on. Had she touched the body or the weapon? Of course not. Why had she called me? Because she was scared, of course. Did she and the victim have a relationship? That made her eyes pop.

"Excuse me?" she nearly shrieked.

"You heard me, Ms. Wren. Were you and the victim intimate?"

She was beet red clear to the roots of her platinum-blond hair. "Of course not. The Louse? Are you kidding me? I admit I don't have great taste in men, but please, give me some credit."

I winced at her tirade. Not a great way to convince the police she was innocent.

"You called him The Louse?" Detective Battersea actually seemed amused by that.

"We all did," she mumbled defensively.

"Why?" He stepped aside so Mr. Voss and his assistant could wheel the gurney by. I tried not to stare at the lumpy black bag sitting on top. Portia kept her eyes glued on Bat.

"Because he was a sexist pig, that's why. He was always grabbing the female employees and volunteers, propositioning them. Sometimes he'd even do it to tourists, which is no way to run a museum. He was mean to his wife, rude to his son, and a total jerk to Roger."

"Roger?" Bat asked.

"Roger Collins. The assistant director here at Flavel House," Portia informed him.

I knew Roger. At least I knew of Roger. He sometimes frequented Sip on Friday evenings where he'd sit in the corner by himself nursing a glass of pinot noir. He was a sad little man with a hangdog expression and a fondness for tweed jackets with or without leather patches on the elbows. That The Louse would be mean to a man like Roger came as no surprise to me. Nixon had probably found him easy prey.

"And what about you, Ms. Wren?" he asked.

I narrowed my eyes. I didn't like the tone of his voice.

Portia looked confused. "What about me?"

"Was he inappropriate with you?"

She rolled her eyes. "He was inappropriate with everyone."

"You didn't answer my question."

"Fine!" she snapped. "Yes. He was sometimes inappropriate."

"In what way?"

She grimaced. "Nothing too obvious. He'd make lewd comments and sometimes brush up against me and pretend it was an accident. That sort of thing."

I knew Portia was underplaying it, but I couldn't blame her. Admitting The Louse had gotten handsy mere hours before his murder wouldn't exactly make Portia look innocent. I mean, I knew she was, but the detective didn't know her like I did, and I had experience with detectives jumping to incorrect conclusions where murder was concerned.

After several more minutes of questioning, Bat turned to me. "How about you? Did you see or hear anything tonight?"

It was my turn under the spotlight. "No. Like I said, Portia called me after she found the body. He was dead when I got here."

"And did you have any run-ins with the victim?"

I propped my hands on my hips. "If you mean did he make lewd comments or put his hands where he shouldn't, then no. I only met the man once at a cocktail party. He was with his wife at the time, so I doubt he was willing to letch in front of her."

"Uh, sure." He looked vaguely uncomfortable at my word usage. "Well, we'll know more once we finish fingerprinting the crime scene. You ladies are free to go. For now."

He didn't quite tell us not to leave town, but it was implied. As was the "or else" that would have naturally come after. I wasted no time dragging Portia down the stairs and out into the now dark streets of Astoria. The grand Victorian manor loomed above us in the dark, its single tower looking downright spooky.

"I can't believe he's dead," Portia whispered as we hustled toward her building. She was clearly still in shock. "Why would someone kill him?"

"The Louse? You mean other than the fact he was harassing half the population of Astoria?"

She let out a strangled laugh. "You exaggerate."

"Not by much. Come on." I wrapped an arm around her shoulders. "Let's get you home before you fall down."

She glanced back at the museum. More windows were lit up now, and I could see figures going in and out. Crime-scene techs, no doubt.

"That detective freaked me out. Do you think he believed me?"

"Of course he did," I assured her. "You were telling the truth. I'm sure he knows it." I wasn't sure of any such thing, but I didn't want her worrying. She sighed in relief. "Good."

But deep in the pit of my stomach, I had a really bad feeling.

☐

Chapter 3

"Portia's in jail."

"Wh—" I rolled over and squinted at the clock. "Do you know what time it is, Cheryl Delaney?"

"Of course I do. It's six in the morning. Now, did you hear me?"

I blinked blearily at the sunlight leaking around the edges of my blinds. I probably should get some curtains. I had pretty, lacy things, but they did nothing to stop the dreaded morning sun. I tried to focus on what Cheryl had said. Last night had been a late one. Portia and I had stayed up past midnight, chatting and laughing and sharing a medicinal bottle of wine. I'd only left after she fell asleep on the couch.

I sat bolt upright in bed. "What happened?"

"I'm not sure. Agatha called me. Said the police had been to Portia's place and dragged her away in handcuffs."

Agatha was Portia's next-door neighbor. She also happened to part of the bunco group Cheryl and I played with every month. Not only that, but she was best friends with Cheryl's mom, which is probably why she'd called Cheryl with the juicy gossip. She knew Cheryl and Portia were friends.

I could hear Cheryl's coffeemaker gurgling through the phone. Coffee. That was the ticket. I staggered out of bed, nearly falling on my face as my feet got tangled in the duvet drooping over the edge of the bed. I staggered through the house, floorboards creaking beneath my feet, intent on making the strongest caffeinated beverage humanly possible. To say I am not a morning person was to, perhaps, under-exaggerate.

"Okay," I said as I snapped one of those pod thingies into the coffeemaker. "Tell me everything." I sank down at the tiny bistro table that sat in the breakfast nook just off the kitchen where my laptop lay neglected. I gave it a glare before turning my gaze to the window. It gave me a nice view of my backyard, which was in desperate need of some TLC. Although the riot of daffodils and hyacinths did distract one from the weeds somewhat.

I loved my little Victorian cottage. It was the first thing I bought when I started making decent money as a writer. It had needed some work, but the place spoke to me, so I'd painted pale yellow with blue and pink trim exactly as it had been when the house had first been built. I had the floors redone and some windows fixed and generally made the place my own. It wasn't as fussy as some of the houses, a little more on the simple side, but it suited me. Alas, I was not much of a gardener. I made a mental note to call one of the local guys to come over and work his magic.

"There's nothing to tell," Cheryl insisted. "All I know is what I just told you."

"Oh, come on." I rescued my mug from beneath the coffeemaker and splashed in a liberal dose of vanilla creamer. "Agatha is a world-class gossip. Surely she gave you more than that." I rested my feet on the other chair and leaned back to enjoy my beverage. Nirvana.

Cheryl sighed, and I could hear her sipping on her own coffee. "Very well. But you didn't hear this from me. And you can't go off half-cocked."

"Sure. Whatever."

"Promise me, Viola."

It was my turn to sigh. "All right. Just tell me."

"According to one of the officers on the scene, the police have hard evidence that Portia killed Mr. Nixon."

# # #

The lobby of the Astoria Police Department was pretty typical, at least from what I'd seen on crime shows. Not the flashy, fictional types, but the real-life stuff on Investigation Discovery Channel. I was mildly addicted to Homicide Hunter. Off-white lino smudged with black scuffs from the bottom of police-issue shoes, off-gray walls that were at once glaring and depressing, photos of retired and/or fallen police officers lining the walls, flickering fluorescents the ratcheted up the headache to migraine proportions. Rather grim. They seriously needed to have a discussion with their interior decorator.

At some point in the distant past, someone had made a half-hearted attempt to lighten up the place. There was a fake fichus in one corner, its droopy plastic leaves coated in dust. Above it hung an equally dusty photograph of the Astoria Column.

Directly across from the glass entry doors was a faux-wood desk topped with bulletproof Plexiglas. The on-duty officer was perched safely behind the glass, a tiny speaker turning her voice into a tinny, crackly mess. She was young, no more than twenty-five, with curly, dark hair twisted into a bun. Her bronze nametag read "Bilson." Neither she nor the name were familiar.

Behind her, a portable room divider blocked the view of what I assumed was the bullpen. It also did double duty as a bulletin board, peppered with pinned notices and reminders.

I rapped on the Plexiglas, and she looked up from the magazine she was flipping through. "How may I help you?" She looked bored. I couldn't blame her. Not a lot happened in Astoria, especially during the off-season when the tourists from Portland stayed home to avoid the excessive amounts of rain on the coast.

I gave her what I considered to be my most charming smile. "I'm here to see Bat. I mean, Detective Battersea."

She was unimpressed. She strummed long, red nails on her desk. "In regards to?"

"The arrest of Portia Wren."

She gave me a blank look. Surely she wasn't that dim. I tried again.

"The murder of August Nixon."

This time she perked up. "Is that what her name is? I hadn't heard." She shot a glare over her shoulder at some unseen person no doubt out of sight behind the divider. "Idiots won't tell me anything. I'll see if Battersea is available." She picked up a black phone that looked about the same vintage as my high school yearbook. Tapping out the numbers, she waited with pursed lips until someone answered on the other end. I couldn't hear what she said, but she put down the phone with a nod and leaned closer to her mic. "He'll be right up. Have a seat."

I nodded and searched for said seat. The only chairs available had cracked, peeling faux-leather cushions marked with stains of dubious origin. I decided to stand.

It was a good ten minutes before Bat finally showed himself. By then, steam was roiling from my ears, and I wished like anything that I wouldn't get thrown in jail for the epic rant I wanted to deliver I stiffened my spine and shot him a death glare, which he promptly ignored. He was dressed in a black suit with a pale-blue shirt and the exact same tie he'd been wearing the day before. Did the man only own one tie? He clutched a cup of coffee in his left hand, steam trailing from the hole in the brown lid. I sniffed. Not coffee. It was definitely tea. Chai, if the spicy scent was anything to go by. That was unexpected. He took a long, slow sip before speaking.

"Good morning, Ms. Roberts. This is a rather early surprise."

I snorted. "According to the rumor mill, you've arrested Portia Wren for Nixon's murder. Is that true?"

One dark brow lifted. "The rumor mill is surprisingly fast. Yes, we arrested Ms. Wren this morning."

"Are you nuts?" I blurted, propping my fists on my ample hips. "Portia is one of the nicest, sweetest people you'll ever meet. There is no way she killed Nixon, no matter how big a louse he was."

He gave me a long, slow look that I couldn't interpret. "I'm afraid the evidence says otherwise."

I glared at him. "What evidence?"

He smirked, and a dimple flashed at the corner of his mouth. "Good try, but you know I can't discuss an ongoing investigation."

"Wait a minute. What about the wineglass? That wasn't Portia's lipstick on it. And she doesn't drink anything but chardonnay. Someone else was there. That person could have killed Nixon."

He paused a beat. "Thank you for your time, Ms. Roberts." And with that, he turned and strode off, the slick leather soles of his dress shoes making a smart sound on the linoleum floor. I tried to refrain, but I couldn't help grinding my teeth. I needed to know what they had on Portia if I was going to show them the error of their ways.

"Pain in the butt, isn't he?" The desk officer had come out from behind the glass. She clutched an e-cigarette in her hand. Smoke break. "Hot, though. Even if he is an old guy."

I wasn't sure that late forties denoted "old," but I mumbled agreement. She was right on all counts. I eyed the desk officer. Maybe she had the information I needed.

"Have you worked with him long? Detective Battersea?" I asked innocently.

She giggled at the thought of her working with the lead detective. "I just started three months ago. I haven't got to work with him. Yet."

I leaned a little closer, lowering my voice conspiratorially. "Give it time. A person with your intelligence and drive is sure to climb the ladder in no time."

"You think?" She beamed at the idea.

I nodded sagely. "I'm rarely wrong about these things." I tapped the side of my nose as if I could smell her success in the air. What I smelled was stale coffee breath. Girl needed a stick of gum.

She held the door open for me, and we both exited into the rare sunny day. In a state known for its rain, Astoria got more than its fair share.

"I wonder what they have on her," I mused out loud.

The officer started up her cig and took a puff. "What they have on who?"

"You know. The woman they brought in. For murder. Portia Wren."

"Oh, her. The one you were talking to the detective about? Something about fingerprints." Her eyes widened as she realized her slip. "You didn't hear that from me, though, okay? I don't think I'm supposed to tell you."

"Tell me what?" I batted my lashes.

She grinned. "Thanks. I'd hate to lose my job so soon. Especially after last time."

"Last time?" "Used to work down at the Safeway," she explained, pointing vaguely in a northerly direction. "I accidentally short-changed a customer. I didn't mean to.

27

It was an honest mistake, but he complained, and they had to let me go." She looked sad for a moment, then perked up. "Lucky my uncle is friends with the chief. He was able to get me this job, so I better not screw it up."

"Oh, I'm certain you won't. I think you're quite good at it. Very professional."

She smiled at me through a cloud of vapor. "Thanks."

"I don't suppose you know any more about the fingerprints? Like, what they were on, for instance?"

"I shouldn't be telling you this, but you're a nice lady and I know she's your friend. I also know what it is to be kept in the dark just because you're new. And female." She gave a snort of disgust then glanced around before leaning closer. I could smell the sweet scent of cloves in her smoke, which was marginally better than coffee breath. "It was the statue. The one of some Greek god or something. They found it next to the body, and Portia Wren's fingerprints were the only ones on it."

☐

Chapter 4

"I can't believe they think Portia capable of murder. I've only met her a few times, but she's a lovely girl. Then again, darkness can lurk in the most unexpected places."

I jerked my cell phone away from my ear and glared at it, even though I knew Lucas couldn't see me. Was he serious? Slapping it back against my ear, I practically shouted, "Listen to me, Lucas Salvatore. Portia did not kill that...jerk. There is no doubt in my mind. And you can take your 'darkness' and...and...shove it."

It was a dumb idea to call Lucas. I thought he'd be supportive. After all, he'd totally had my back at the writer's conference in Florida. Plus we were dating. Kind of. I was hesitant to call him my boyfriend. It seemed like such a juvenile word. Right now, though, his name was mud.

"Hey, hey," he soothed, his voice a rich baritone in my ear. "I didn't mean to upset you, but you know as well as I do that people can surprise you. They can be very good at keeping secrets."

"Not Portia." Though a seed of doubt had already niggled its way into my brain, which annoyed me to death. No. Portia was innocent of The Louse's murder. Of that I had no doubt. Some people thought she was snobby or whatever because she always dressed like a runway model rather than in jeans and flannel shirts, but she was a sweetheart. She happened to like pretty clothes and dressing up. What was wrong with that?

"I hope you're right."

"Of course I am," I snapped. "I was right last time, wasn't I?" Last time being when I found a dead body on the beach in Florida, and Cheryl and I ended up suspects. Fun times.

"Speaking of last time, maybe you shouldn't get involved this go 'round. You nearly got yourself killed. Perhaps you should step back and let the police handle it."

I snorted. "As if. I'm not letting my friend rot in jail any longer than necessary just because the police think they know something." I turned on the tap and rinsed out my coffee mug. "They have no evidence."

He cleared his throat. "Fingerprints on the weapon seem like a pretty solid piece of evidence."

"Sure. They seem that way," I admitted. I swung open the fridge door and stared inside. Empty. I hadn't had time to go grocery shopping what with my deadline and everything. "But these things can be faked, you know."

"It's true," he admitted. "But according to my research, in most instances—"

"Listen, I've got to go," I said, cutting him off. I didn't want to hear anything negative from him. It would only piss me off. "Need to hunt down some lipstick."

"That's a new one."

I laughed. "I'll tell you all about it later. By the way, when are you headed this way next?" I fidgeted with the blue and white dish towel hanging from the fridge handle.

"I was thinking I'd come by this weekend. We could have some dinner. Maybe a bottle of wine. If you're not too busy trying to solve another mystery."

"We'll see," I said slyly. "If you're lucky."

# # #

There were exactly five places in Astoria a woman could buy cosmetics. For inexpensive to downright cheap stuff, there was the local grocery store and two independent pharmacies. The selections were small and the prices exorbitant. Then there were two salons that sold higher-end cosmetics. Based on the neon-pink color of the lipstick on the second wineglass, I was guessing cheap. But then, I tended toward neutrals, so what did I know?

I hoped that if I could find out who carried lipstick that color, I might be able to find out who bought it. That particularly shocking shade of pink hadn't been popular since the eighties, so I couldn't imagine too many women in Astoria wearing it. I hadn't found it online, so I was hoping I'd have better luck in person. Maybe it was a fool's errand, but I had to try.

A quick stop at the grocery yielded nothing. They had six colors, none of which matched the picture on my phone. I had equally disappointing results with the drugstores. The first of the two salons, however, showed promise.

The salon was in one of the storefronts along Commercial Street, the main drag of downtown Astoria.

The three-story brick building had been built sometime at the turn of the last century. More recently the brick had been painted white. Large front windows were filled with spa-like elements from river rocks meant for hot-stone massage to tiers of candles in glass globes. Swirling letters proclaimed it to be Viviana's Salon and Cosmetics. I pushed the door open and stepped inside to the pungent odor of hair products and too much perfume. My eyes began watering immediately. My head throbbed in time to the beat from the radio. Something catchy and fun. Unless you had a headache.

The girl behind the front desk, which looked more like a podium than an actual desk, glanced at me through eyes lined with thick, black kohl. Her pale-blond hair was artfully wispy with a bubblegum-pink streak over her left ear, which matched her pink and white striped shirt and pink combat boots. Her skinny jeans had artful rips in interesting places.

"Welcome to Viviana's. How may we enhance your beauty today?" she chirped perkily, though her eyes were glazed with boredom. Or pot. Who knew around here?

"I'm looking for lipstick."

"Oh, sure. Over here." She tromped to a display of makeup only marginally more extensive than the drug and grocery stores. "We carry Viviana's own line of mineral makeup. Non-toxic. All natural. So good for your skin." She waved to one of the shelves, her pink, glittery nails flashing in the light streaming through the window. "Lipstick. What color?"

"Pink. Bright pink."

That startled a response out of her. She eyed me doubtfully. "Are you sure?"

I stared her down. "Of course. Why?"

"Just, um, it's not the right color for you."

I scrambled for an excuse. The bonus of hitting the other stores was that nobody cared. They were totally anonymous. I could browse the makeup section without anyone batting an eyelash or asking silly questions about my color choices. "It's for my mom. She loves bright pink."

"Ohh!" The girl's eyes widened as if it suddenly all made sense. "I have noticed older ladies tend to like bright colors." She snagged a couple of tubes from the shelf. "These are our brightest."

I took them from her and slipped off the lids. One was a shocking purplish color, and the other more of a raspberry. Neither of them were anything like the lipstick on the glass.

"This is all you've got? No pink?"

She shrugged. "Sorry."

"Thanks anyway."

The other salon was a few doors down from Viviana's, but it was closed. It looked like a one-woman operation with a note on the door explaining that it was by appointment only. I couldn't see any makeup on the display inside, so I was betting it was mail-order only.

I was having zero luck with the lipstick hunt, and my feet were starting to hurt. It was nearing lunchtime, and I was running on coffee fumes, so I decided to head to the bakery for a sandwich and more caffeination. Then I should get home and do some work.

I'd decided to swap to a different work-in-progress since I was having fits with Scarlet and Rolf. In The Rancher's Virgin Bride, Matilda had run away from her evil, murderous husband back east and into the arms of the hot, sexy cattle rancher, Blade. Unfortunately, Blade thought Matilda was a nun. I had all kinds of interesting ideas about how to get her out of that conundrum. At least two of which involved ropes and lacy undergarments. I smirked to myself. A writer's work was never done.

I was in my car, headed to the bakery, when the Flavel House loomed up on my left. I paused, and, without thinking, pulled my car over in front of the museum. Cardamom scones could wait. Maybe there was something yet to be learned inside the scene of the crime.

☐

Chapter 5

One of Portia's coworkers at the museum was a young woman with the unfortunate name of Annabelle Smead. Not that Annabelle was an unfortunate name, but Smead?

I knew little about her, except that she was a single mother and had a penchant for wearing sack-like dresses in ghastly colors that clashed with her bright-red hair. What we called "carrot" back in school, but a kinder person might call "sunset."

She jumped up from one of the armchairs the moment I walked in the front door. "Oh, Viola! Did you hear about Portia?" she blurted. She was even paler than usual, making her freckles stand out like big, brown spots. She wrung her boney hands together repeatedly. Clearly the whole mess had gotten to her.

"I did," I assured her, noting the crime-scene tape that crisscrossed the closed doors to the study. That section was definitely off the tour today. "I went to the police station this morning."

Annabelle's blue eyes grew wide. "So you saw her? She's okay?"

"No. They won't let anyone in but her lawyer. I'm sure she's fine, though. She's strong." This was Astoria, after all. Not Portland. She likely had the entire jail to herself, and they were probably feeding her fast food. Which she might consider torture, but most people would be happy with.

"Oh, she is. Such a strong woman. I admire her so much."

Good. That was something I could work with.

"Do you think she killed The L— uh, Mr. Nixon?" I asked.

She rolled her eyes and plopped down in her armchair. There was a book sitting on the end table next to her. I noticed it was a newly released crime novel borrowed from the library down the street. "Give me a break. That girl wouldn't hurt a fly."

"Good. My sentiments exactly." I glanced around, but the place seemed empty. "Is it all right to talk?"

"Sure." She fidgeted, sorting stacks of brochures. "This time of day, the place is pretty empty. Have a seat."

"Okay." I sat down on a wooden chair across the hall from her. There was a red velvet cushion on it to match the loveseat and chairs clustered up and down the hall. "I was hoping you could help me."

"Me?" She seemed surprised.

I nodded. "I'm trying to help Portia, and I was wondering if you knew anything. Anything at all. About the murder, I mean."

"Oh, no. The police asked, but I don't know anything. I have no idea who would murder Mr. Nixon or why."

"Other than the fact he was a letch?"

Her cheeks blazed. "He was, rather unfortunately, not a nice man in that area, but I can't imagine someone murdering him over it."

Other than his wife, maybe. Wives were often displeased by philandering husbands.

"Good point," I said, going along with her assessment for the moment. "What about the night he died? Did he have any visitors? Appointments?" Maybe Annabelle knew who the pink-lipstick wearer was. I noticed she wore a nude shade of lipgloss, so it likely wasn't her. If the salon girl thought I'd look bad in pink lipstick, she should meet Annabelle.

"Oh, yes, he had an appointment that night at six. I don't know who, though. He put it on the calendar himself. We all sync our calendars, but we're responsible for our own appointments."

"Can you look?"

She shrugged. "If it will help Portia."

"It will."

She nodded and pulled her cell phone out of her purse. A few swipes on the screen later, she gave a triumphant smile. "Here it is. Six p.m. Mrs. A."

"Do you know who Mrs. A is?"

"Sorry, I don't." She looked ready to cry.

"It's okay. I'll figure it out." Maybe. I rubbed the bridge of my nose, trying to think. "So, were you here the night of the murder?"

"Oh, no. My son was ill. I stayed home that day to take care of him."

"Sorry to hear that. Hope he's okay."

She gave me a tremulous smile. "He'll be fine." She didn't sound convinced. I felt badly for her, but I was more concerned with Portia at the moment.

"Anything else? Did Mr. Nixon have an argument with anyone recently?"

She blanched again. "The police asked that too. And I'm sorry, but I had to tell them."

"Tell them what?"

Annabelle swallowed. "That the day he died, Mr. Nixon had a violent argument with someone and that person threatened to kill him."

A feeling of dread pooled in my stomach. "Who was it?"

"Portia Wren."

# # #

"How do you know Annabelle is telling the truth?" Cheryl asked as she scooped up a forkful of salad. She'd agreed to meet me for lunch, even though she was on a deadline for her latest thriller. Like me, Cheryl was a novelist. Unlike me, there was no bodice-ripping in her books, and she wasn't cursed with writer's block. "She could have lied, you know."

"She could have," I admitted. "It would be an easy enough thing to fake. And with only the kid to corroborate. But still, I got the feeling she was being genuine."

"You and your gut feelings. What was it this time?" She munched on the rabbit food with gusto. I couldn't stand salads. Even if they were smothered in hunks of bleu cheese and slices of fried chicken.

I set down my turkey Reuben and ruminated on it. "Her reaction when I asked her about anyone who might have threatened Nixon. When she told me about Portia, she was practically in tears."

"Could have been faking."

I shrugged and took a sip of root beer. "I suppose, but I honestly think she was telling the truth."

"Okay, so maybe she was." Cheryl switched into devil's advocate mode. "It's possible she was trying to make Portia look bad. Shift the blame. I mean, Annabelle could have had a motive herself, you know."

I frowned. "You think The Louse was harassing her, too?"

"It's a possibility." She took another bite of her salad. It was peppered with slivers of almonds and chunks of dried cranberry. If they put that in a muffin, I'd be all over it.

"Okay, I can see that. She's pretty, and Nixon was, well, a louse. Plus she's super mousey, and he delighted in bullying people he deemed weaker than him. But I can't see her killing him over it. She's timid. Not like Portia."

"Not ballsy, you mean?" Cheryl said dryly.

I cleared my throat and held back a laugh. "Exactly."

"She could have another motive. Something that was worth killing for."

I chewed a big bite of the Reuben. "I'll bite. What sort of motive would Annabelle have that would get a timid thing like her riled enough to kill a man?"

"Is she married?"

"Nope. No man in the picture, as far as I can tell. Just the kid."

"And she said he was sick?"

I nodded. "If I recall correctly, Portia once mentioned the kid was sick a lot. Something chronic maybe."

"So, what if she wanted time off and he wouldn't give it to her?"

I snorted. "Wouldn't she just quit?"

"Maybe. Unless she was too afraid of not having a job." I shook my head. "I can't picture that one. What about money? Maybe he wasn't paying her for some reason?"

"That would make me murderous," Cheryl said, wadding up her napkin and tossing it on the table. "What if the money she was making wasn't enough?"

I frowned. "To take care of her and her son, you mean?"

"Right. Illness is expensive in this country. A single mom with a sick kid and probably the most basic insurance? Bound to get spendy."

"You think she killed him because she wanted a raise?"

"Well, no, of course not, but money is often a motive, right?"

She was right about that. "I guess she could have been doing something illegal to make money, and he caught on. She killed him to shut him up."

Cheryl frowned. "But what, though? Pot brownies maybe?"

I laughed. "Not exactly illegal anymore."

"Yeah, but she probably isn't licensed, and I doubt you can sell them out of a museum."

"But still not worth killing over. I think you're on to something, though. I'm going to look into the money angle some more. After my next stop."

"Where are you off to next?"

"Roger Collins, assistant director of the Flavel House Museum. I'd like to hear what he has to say about The Louse."

"Good luck. I'm off to hunt down a serial killer."

I grinned. "I think you're the one that needs the luck."

"No kidding," she sighed. "You have no idea how hard it is to leave a trail of bodies interspersed with red herrings."

I wasn't so sure about that. I was getting far too familiar with both of those things.

# # #

As soon as I left the bakery, I dialed the number Annabelle had given me for Roger Collins. According to her, he'd called in sick to work that morning, leaving her to run the place alone. Not exactly a glowing character recommendation in my book. Still, it would hopefully make it easier to question him, since he would be relaxed on his own turf and not distracted by work.

The phone rang several times before an automated voice instructed me to leave a message. I didn't bother. This was something better done face to face anyway.

Collins lived mere blocks from the bakery in a Craftsman cottage halfway up the hill. It was painted an unfortunate shade of peach which clashed with the red brick of the chimney. A porch swing swayed slightly in the light spring breeze, and a few daffodils and crocuses bravely lifted their heads toward the early afternoon sun. Or what was left of it. Clouds had begun to scuttle in from the north, and the air had taken on a slight chill.

I rapped on the front door. Not so much as a whisper from inside. Maybe he hadn't heard. I rang the bell. Still nothing.

There was a garage to the side of the house, so I made my way down the porch steps and walked around the house. Standing on tiptoes, I peered into the garage. Dim shapes huddled under bright-blue tarps. I couldn't tell if it was furniture or what, but it definitely wasn't a car. Apparently the terribly sick Mr. Collins was off running around somewhere.

I'd have to catch him later. Preferably when he least expected it.

I returned to my car, frustrated but determined. Something white fluttering on the windshield caught my eye. With a frown, I plucked the piece of paper from under the wiper blade. Surely it wasn't a parking ticket. There wasn't a sign anywhere on the street.

As I read the note, my eyes widened. It wasn't a ticket. It was a message. Block letters spelled out:

BE CAREFUL. CURIOSITY KILLED THE CAT.

☐

Shéa MacLeod

Chapter 6

The Prohibition was an ironic name for a bar and restaurant known for its pre-Prohibition cocktails. It thoroughly embraced the aesthetics of the era in every aspect. From the fire glowing in the hearth to the twang of the old-timey music, the Edison light bulbs, and the American flag draped off the corner of one of the shelves behind the bar. Shelves crammed with liquors I'd never even heard of like Boodles British Gin. There was even an absinthe dispenser, which I found interesting, but I never touched the stuff. Black licorice is one of the most disgusting flavors on Earth, as far as I'm concerned.

Lucas and I perched ourselves at the bar, so we could get the scoop from the cheerful bartender. She greeted us with a smile and answered our questions about the drinks. I chose Rival #7. Mostly because it involved maraschino cherries, which are delicious, and rye whiskey, which is almost as good as blackberry bourbon. Lucas chose a Lightship #50, which sounded good because of the apple brandy, until the bartender informed us there was a "splash of absinthe." Thanks, but no thanks.

I grinned happily to myself, enjoying the chill atmosphere and the fact that Lucas was back in town. I didn't want to admit to myself that I'd missed him. Just a little. Friday evening hadn't come fast enough.

I hadn't told Lucas or anyone else about the note on my car. It wasn't a threat—not exactly. Okay, so it was a threat, but not a specific one. Probably some nosey neighbor or something. Sure. And I've got a bridge in Arizona for sale. I didn't want anyone freaking out. I could handle this myself. Until I knew who left the note, there was no point getting everyone riled up.

"So, catch me up on what's been going on?" Lucas asked, sipping his Lightship.

I sighed. "Well, I've been struggling with this scene in my book. Scarlet lied to Rolf and he found out. Was totally pissed, of course, but I've no idea what the lie was. Ridiculous really. It's what I get for not plotting everything out ahead of time." Some authors were "plotters." They planned out the whole book before they even started writing. Some were "pantsers." They wrote randomly whatever spewed out of their brains on a given day and worried about tying it all up later. Me, I was somewhere in the middle. I'd have a plot, more or less, but would wing a lot of it. Which potentially led to a conundrum now and then. Like the one with Scarlet and Rolf. "I actually switched books and started working on something else, hoping it would jar the old creative juices. No such luck. Got stuck on that one, too."

"I'm sorry you're stuck, but you know that isn't what I meant," he said, giving me a look.

I heaved a sigh. Of course I did. I took a fortifying sip of whiskey-flavored goodness and dove in. I told him about my search for the lipstick, my visit with Annabelle, and the fact that I hadn't been able to find Roger Collins.

"Maybe he'll be at the memorial service tomorrow. I can question him then."

Lucas shook his head. "I don't know why you think the police can't handle this."

"Because it's pretty obvious they can't. Portia did not kill anyone. She's just not the type."

He eyed me carefully. "Everyone's the type, Viola. You know that. Given the right motive, even you could commit murder."

I snorted. "Yeah, but I'm not nearly as nice a person as Portia."

He grinned. "I enjoy your sassy ways." Then he sobered. "I just worry."

"I know you do. And I appreciate it, but everything is under control."

He looked dubious, but didn't say anything more. I took that as a good sign.

"You could help me, you know."

"If I can, I will. You know that."

I did, but I wasn't used to this "being able to rely on a man" business. Most of my adult life had been spent on my own, and I liked it that way. I hadn't expected Lucas to throw a monkey wrench into the situation.

He ordered another round, and we chatted about mundane things: our books, deadlines, upcoming travel. He was headed to Phoenix in two weeks for a thriller writers' convention. I was going to San Diego in the summer for a romance novelists' conference. We talked about attending a conference in Florida again, but this time together.

As the night stretched on, the whiskey went to my head, despite the addition of marinated olives, hush puppies, and a charcuterie plate. I had no idea if the food was pre-Prohibition, too, but I doubted it. In any case, it was delicious.

I started thinking about ways to free Portia. Maybe if I could get Bat's focus off Portia and on to someone else...

Yes, that was it.

Lucas interrupted my train of thought. "What is your devious mind planning now?"

"Oh, nothing," I said tipsily. "But I think it might be time to head home."

He nodded and paid for dinner and drinks before helping me with my coat. He walked me home but didn't ask to come in, and I didn't invite him. It wasn't that I didn't want him to, but I wasn't quite ready for that. Plus I had plans.

"See you tomorrow, Viola," he said softly before bending down to kiss me.

It was a thorough kiss. A swoony kiss. I very nearly lost my balance and toppled off the porch. I stood there for a long time watching him as his car disappeared into the night. Then I shook my head. I had plans to see to. What did old Sherlock say?

The game is afoot!

# # #

The next morning, I woke rather fuzzy-brained and disoriented. The pale-blue ceiling came swimming into view, the ornate medallion in the middle from which the chandelier hung finally pulling into focus. My head was throbbing slightly, and my mouth felt like cotton wool. I rarely overindulged—moderation and all that—but apparently those cocktails were stronger than I realized.

I wondered if I should have invited Lucas in after all. I'd hate for him to think I wasn't interested, but I refused to bow to pressure just because of someone else's time scale. I wasn't even sure Lucas cared about time scales. We were doing our own thing, and he seemed fine with it. I think.

I groaned. Thinking hurt my brain. I needed coffee. Lots of it. And then I needed to sit my butt at my computer for a couple hours and get some work done before the memorial service...

I froze.

Memories of the night before flooded my mind. Lucas walking me to the front door. Lucas kissing me. Lucas driving away. Me going inside the house...

No, I didn't go inside. Instead I drove to Detective Battersea's place and left a note on the windshield of his car. A murder confession.

"Oh, crap." I rolled over and buried my face in the pillow. I'd lost my ever-loving mind. Why did I think leaving a murder confession on a cop's car was a good idea? Granted, it was anonymous, but still. He could totally do a handwriting analysis or fingerprint it or something, and he'd figure out it was me.

No, wait. He'd have to have a sample to compare it to, which he didn't. And my fingerprints would have to be on file, which they weren't. So, there was no way he could know I did it, right?

Cheryl would know what to do. Maybe.

I staggered from bed, threw on my fuzzy, blue bathrobe, grabbed my phone, and headed to the kitchen. I needed, like, a thousand gallons of coffee—stat! Unfortunately, standing on my back porch was Detective James Battersea. He was wearing the same yellow and blue tie, and he was holding up my note. With a groan, I tightened my bathrobe belt and swung open the door.

"Viola, you've got some explaining to do."

"I don't know what you're talking about." I tried to look innocent and no doubt failed miserably.

He tapped the note right on the spot where my website was printed along the bottom. I'd used my author stationary? I had lost my mind.

I closed my eyes and let out a huge sigh. "Are you going to arrest me?"

"Maybe not. If you can explain this. And if you have coffee."

"I was about to make some. Come on in."

While Bat sat at my kitchen table and I made coffee for both of us, I explained my thought process regarding the note. "It was stupid. Really stupid," I admitted. "I literally can't believe I did it. But at the time..." I trailed off.

"At the time, it seemed reasonable?"

I sighed. "Yeah. It did. I'm sorry, and I promise I'll never do it again. It's not like me at all. I was just so worried about Portia, and I thought if you had a reason to look elsewhere..." I shrugged and handed him a large mug of black coffee, then I sat down with my own sweet and light.

"You're worried for your friend. I get it," he said, surprisingly sympathetic. "But you've got to let the police handle this. Believe it or not, we do know what we're doing."

"I know. I'm an idiot."

"I'm going to let this go this once, as long as you promise not to do it again. And to let me do my job."

"I promise." It wasn't a lie. I would let him do his job, but I had zero intention of leaving the investigation solely in his hands.

☐

Shéa MacLeod

Chapter 7

"You did what?"

"I know," I admitted as Lucas parked the car on Franklin. "It wasn't my brightest move."

"You could have been arrested."

"I know," I repeated. "I guess too many pre-Prohibition cocktails is a bad idea."

"I guess," he said under his breath. He got out of the car and opened the door for me.

August Nixon's memorial service was held that Saturday, which meant that Lucas was able to play escort. We arrived at the Masonic Lodge—the Nixons weren't churchgoers—suitably dressed in somber colors. Well, somberish. Lucas was sophisticated and elegant in a classic black suit, but the closest thing to a somber color I owned was a cobalt-blue maxi dress.

The lodge had been built in 1923 after the original building burned down, but the Masons had insisted on replicating the gorgeous nineteenth-century building, complete with front columns. It was like a mini White House perched on the side of the hill, elegant and mysterious. Or maybe that was just me.

"Are you sure about this?" Lucas asked, pausing outside the wide double doors. There was a fine mist in the air and droplets clung to his salt-and-pepper hair.

"Why? Scared?" I sniped back, starting to withdraw my hand from the crook of his arm. Why couldn't he just be supportive?

"After last time?" he asked, refusing to let go of my hand. "Of course I am. You nearly died. Twice. I don't relish the thought of it happening again."

His answer mollified me. "I'll be careful. I promise."

He sighed but said nothing more. Really, he was sweet to worry about me, but I could handle myself.

Inside the grand lodge, chairs had been lined up facing the southern end of the room, where an enormous photo of the deceased had been set up on an easel. Massive floral arrangements drowned the floor, crowding out the wooden podium and perfuming the air. The pollen tickled my nose, and I stifled a sneeze. Great. I should have taken my allergy pills today.

People milled about, speaking in hushed tones and casting glances at the smirking picture of the dead man. Either Nixon had a lot of friends or he was in a high enough position in Astoria society that people wanted to be sure they were seen at his service. Call me cynical, but I was betting on the later. This was definitely a "see and be seen" sort of event. No one appeared terribly sad.

Eventually everyone was seated, and the service began. Various pillars of society took turns at the podium, droning on ad naseum about the wonderful qualities of the deceased. Maybe I was the only one who noticed it, but they didn't seem to know the man very well. It was all generalities and butt-kissing interspersed with sympathetic glances at the widow. I tuned them out and focused instead on the attendees, specifically the widow and her son.

Mrs. Nixon was not a young woman, but she had that ageless sort of beauty I associated with Golden Era actresses, such as Lauren Bacall and Audrey Hepburn. She was dressed in a simple black shift that fell just below the knees, sensible but elegant black heels, and a simple strand of white pearls. To ward against the chill of the old building, she'd wrapped a gray silk shawl around her shoulders. The most ostentatious thing about her was the giant rock on her left hand. I wondered if that had been her choice or his. Wedding rings said a lot about people, in my opinion. Based on the rest of her understated outfit, I was betting the ring had been his choice and she wore it because he wanted her to, not because it was her style. I hadn't known Nixon, but he struck me as the type who liked to flash his cash. He'd certainly enjoyed lording it over his underlings, if Portia's stories were anything to go by.

The son looked to be in his early thirties, reasonably attractive, and not terribly thrilled to be there. Although he sat up straight, there was a slight slouch to his shoulders as if he'd like to melt off his chair and away from everything. His sandy hair tumbled into his eyes and curled over his collar, desperately in need of a trim. His suit, although expensive-looking, didn't fit quite right, as if he'd grabbed it off the rack and hadn't bothered with alteration.

Mother and son sat stiffly side by side, neither looking at nor touching each other. Did that mean they weren't close? Or that they were angry with each other? Perhaps they weren't the touchy-feely sorts, or maybe they were fighting over the will. Or what if they knew who killed Nixon!

I fidgeted through the entire service, equal parts bored and anxious. I couldn't wait to get myself in front of Mrs. Nixon and try to worm some information out of her. Subtly, of course.

The minute the service was over, I plowed my way toward the front, Lucas trailing a bit reluctantly, albeit with some amusement. I knew he didn't like me getting involved in a crime again, but tough cookies. It was my friend who was in trouble, and I wouldn't stop until I'd proven her innocence.

"Mrs. Nixon," I burst out, interrupting a middle-aged couple overdressed for the occasion. I gave them an apologetic smile and turned back to my quarry. "I am so sorry to hear about your loss."

"Thank you." Her tone was elegant and cultured, her expression cool and distant. Did rich people practice that look in the mirror?

I squeezed her hand in sympathy. "It must have been such a shock when the police informed you."

"Yes." Her expression gave nothing away.

I scrambled for something else to say. A way to ask questions without being totally obvious. Behind me, Lucas shifted, stretching his hand toward the widow.

"Mrs. Nixon. So sorry for your loss. Lucas Salvatore."

Something in her perked up. "The Lucas Salvatore? The author?"

He had the grace to blush. "Yes. I'm afraid so."

Although outwardly Mrs. Nixon remained calm, her eyes were practically dancing with excitement. Clearly she was a big-time fan.

"Mrs. Nixon..." he began.

"Mary, please."

"Mary." He squeezed her hand, and she actually fluttered her lashes. I managed to hide my amusement, though it wasn't easy. "How did you manage? Hearing about something like that? You must have been devastated."

Oh, the smooth talker. She didn't even know what hit her. I had to admit, Lucas had a way with the ladies. If I were a lesser woman, I'd have been a seething mass of jealousy. As it was, things were working in my favor. Go, Lucas.

"It was such a shock," Mary Nixon agreed. "I couldn't believe it. That, at the very time I was enjoying myself at the movies with friends, my poor dear August was lying dead." She let out a little sob and dabbed at her eyes with a tissue.

I wasn't sure if she was being genuine or having a case of the dramatics. And a movie as an alibi? I'd seen enough Perry Mason to know that could be faked. I wondered how I could finagle her friends' names out of her so I could question them.

"I do hope you had someone to stand by your side." He patted her hand and gave her a look of deep sympathy.

"Oh, yes. Roger Collins was lovely. Took care of everything. That man has been a godsend."

"Oh, please, mother," the son snapped, standing up so abruptly from where he'd been lounging on the folding chair that the chair toppled backward with a crash. People turned to stare, but he ignored them. Instead, he gave his mother a hard glare. "Do you have to be so obvious?"

She touched her strand of pearls, eyes wide. "I don't know what you mean, Blaine."

He snorted in derision. "Sure you don't, mother." He turned and stomped off toward the stairs leading up and out of the ballroom. I gave Lucas a look, hoping he'd interpret that I wanted him to stay and pump Mary Nixon for info while I took off after Blaine Nixon.

Blaine was quick on his feet, I'd give him that. By the time I made it up the stairs, he was nowhere to be seen. He could be in the men's room, which would be a rather awkward situation should I barge in, or...

I shoved open the front door and stepped out onto the porch. Sure enough, Blaine was standing on the front lawn, but he wasn't alone. He was having a loud argument with a balding man wearing an ancient, beige suit and horn-rimmed glasses. The two were shouting at each other like a couple of fishwives. Being the nosey git I am, I moved closer so I could hear better.

"Listen, you old—" (I won't repeat the word Blaine used, but it was quite the insult.) "Get out of here before I call the cops."

"I came to pay my respects, you arrogant waste of flesh. Your father and I may have had our differences, but never let it be said that I didn't observe the proper etiquette."

"That's rich," Blaine sneered. "I don't give a flying—" Again with the language. "Get out of here." He grabbed the older man by the lapel and dragged him across the lawn toward the street. With one hard shove, the older man stumbled off the lodge's property, and Blaine stomped back toward the building. Right before he went inside, he turned and shouted, "You better not show your face again, old man, or you'll regret it."

☐

Chapter 8

The man in the beige suit shot Blaine an angry look before going on his own merry way. I dithered. Should I go after Blaine? Or question the man in the beige suit?

I knew who Blaine was. I could easily track him down and question him later. I had no idea who the older man was or how to find him again. Beige Suit it was.

I hurried across the lawn, heels sinking into the soft soil. Really, I had to get better funeral footwear if I was going to go chasing suspects through rain-softened grass. I made it to the street without breaking an ankle and clattered after Beige Suit as quickly as I could. He must have heard me, because he turned around as I came huffing up to him.

"May I help you?" He seemed only mildly interested.

Bracing my aching side with my palm, I gave him what I hoped was a sympathetic smile. "Viola Roberts. I saw what happened between you and Blaine Nixon. I don't know what sort of history you two have, but I thought he treated you terribly. And I, uh, just wanted to tell you that," I finished lamely.

The smile he gave me was genuine. He was a pleasant-looking older man with a round face and overly exuberant white eyebrows. They sort of made up for the lack of hair on his head. I caught a whiff of Old Spice, which I found quite pleasant. It suited him.

He held out his hand. "Charles Phillips. Pleased to meet you."

We shook hands. "How do you know the Nixons?" I asked.

"I'm their neighbor, actually. Have been for over twenty years."

Color me surprised. Blaine had acted like the man was the anti-Christ. "Well, that was awfully nice of you to show up. I can't believe Blaine was so nasty about it."

He shook his head and gave a little sigh. "Not really his fault, poor boy. His father and I never got along, you see."

"I see. And yet you still came to the service. That's quite mature of you." I nearly smacked myself in the head. Of course it was mature. The man must be near on to seventy. He'd better be mature by now.

Charles Phillips chuckled, not at all offended by my gaffe. "I do try."

"Can I ask why you didn't get along? Was it because Nixon was The Louse?"

His grin widened. "Is that what they call him?" He appeared incredibly cheered by the thought.

I returned his smile. "Well, that's what the women who worked with him called him. Because, well, he wasn't a nice man."

"Grabby," Phillips said as if he knew what he was talking about. "Not just about women, either."

I raised an eyebrow. "Really?"

He turned and began to stroll down Franklin Street, hands clasped behind his back. "That's what our feud was about. You see, I inherited my house from my mother. My father built it shortly after World War II."

"Wow. That's impressive."

"It was how things were often done back then. And my father was a master craftsman."

"Even more impressive. So, what happened? With Nixon, I mean."

"Well, when the Nixons moved in, August immediately had the land resurveyed. Turns out, the fence which had been put in several decades earlier was actually partially on his property."

"But possession is nine-tenths of the law or something, right?" I'd read that somewhere. Property laws often broke down to who was actually making use of the land, regardless of what old documents said. The neighbors simply signed an agreement, perhaps a changed a token amount of money, and everything was hunky dory.

"You'd think so," Mr. Phillips agreed, "and I thought that would be the case. And after months of expensive lawyers and court visits, it looked like it was going my way."

"I'm guessing it didn't."

"We'll never know," he said grimly. "One night, August rammed his car into the fence, taking half of it out in one fell swoop."

"Crikey!"

"Indeed. It wasn't that I cared so much about the land or the fence, but my mother had planted some beautiful rosebushes along the fence after my father died. She cared for them like they were her babies. If things went against me, I planned to relocate them, but August never gave me a chance."

"He destroyed the roses?"

"Every one of them."

"Gosh, I'm sorry. That sucks."

"It does," he admitted. "And it led to a decades-long feud with my neighbor."

"You couldn't forgive him?" I asked.

"Oh, that wasn't the problem. He sued me for damage to his car."

"What a jerk!" I couldn't believe what I was hearing. Or rather, I could. August Nixon had been a big, fat louse. Worse than a louse. "Do the police know about your feud? Because they might decide you're a suspect." Though I couldn't see him being a killer.

"Oh, they know," he said with a wave of his hand. "But I have an alibi."

"Well, that's good. Especially if you can prove it easily." I hoped he'd get my nudge.

"Oh, believe me, I can."

I waited. Surely he'd tell me.

"I was at the police station."

# # #

"Seriously?" Cheryl asked, eyes wide. Her hair was spikier than usual and...

Was she wearing glitter? Naw, I had to be imagining it.

"That's what Charles Phillips said. He was in the middle of reporting some kids for vandalism. I double checked with Bilson, the duty clerk, and she confirmed it."

Cheryl and I were sitting with Nina at her wine bar, enjoying a late afternoon glass of wine. Outside, it was raining in earnest. Lucas had left straight after the memorial, as he had a reading at Powell's Books in Portland the next day.

"Vandalism?" Nina asked. "In Astoria?" She sounded amused. "What did they do? TP his front lawn?"

"Actually," I smirked, "that's exactly what they did."

Nina chortled. Cheryl shook her head and said, "You gotta love small towns. But I guess that means we can cross Charles Phillips off the suspect list."

I nodded. "The police sure have. It's pretty obvious. Hard to be in two places at once, and it doesn't get much better of an alibi than a police station."

"No kidding." Nina leaned against the bar and reached over to top off my glass. Pinot noir today. "Well, I'm sorry I missed old August's memorial. Bet it was a hoot."

"It was certainly interesting," I admitted. I'd left out the detail about me getting drunk the night before the memorial service and leaving a note on Bat's police vehicle. I already felt like a big enough idiot.

"I'm relieved you talked Lucas into going instead of me," Cheryl said. "I hate memorial services. Plus that looming deadline." She stared forlornly into her glass.

"Don't tell me you're blocked, too," I said. It happened to the best of us. Not in the way people talked about, like you had no idea what to write. More like, you got stuck in a plot. You weren't sure which way to move or what should happen next. How to connect point D to point J, as it were. It always happened. Every time. Every book. It was always to be expected, and always frustrating. Usually for me, the best way to shake it was to do something else. Something random and new. Or something fun and enjoyable. I'd feel guilty half the time, but it was a necessary part of the creative process. So far, though, it wasn't working.

"Totally," she said, taking a sip. "Stupid Dirk got his stupid butt locked up in a Hungarian prison with no way out."

"Helicopter," I suggested.

She blinked. "What?"

"One of his cohorts could land on the roof with a helicopter and break him out."

"Can't. No one knows he's in Hungary."

"Dynamite." Nina's suggestion.

Cheryl shook her head. "Where would he get it? Not like they have stacks of the stuff lying around in Hungarian prisons."

"Fake illness."

We all stared down at the end of the bar where Lloyd sat in his usual spot, nursing a glass of cheap table wine. He always bought a bottle at a time and never paid more than ten dollars a bottle.

"What are you talking about, Lloyd?" Nina demanded, propping one fist on her hip. She was wearing jeans today with a snug, navy sweater. Her Saturday work uniform.

"Hungary is part of the EU. Got standards, even in prisons. Prisoner gets sick enough, they gotta take him to the hospital, don't they? Then he can escape. Easier from a hospital." Lloyd buried his nose in his glass again.

Cheryl hopped off the stool, dashed to the end of the bar, and planted a big kiss on Lloyd's cheek. "You're a genius," she crowed. Lloyd blushed cherry-tomato red. Cheryl dashed back to her seat and grabbed her purse and jacket. She downed the last of her wine. "Gotta go. I've got a jail break to plan!"

☐

Shéa MacLeod

Chapter 9

I thought about following Cheryl out of the wine bar. I had my own book to write, after all. Plus there was the investigation, not that I had anywhere to go with that. I was pretty much stalled at the moment.

"So, you talked to the wife, huh?" Nina asked, holding up a bottle of Syrah.

Might as well. I gave her the nod, and she filled my glass with rich, red liquid. I took an appreciative sip. Berries and sunshine and maybe a hint of chocolate. Heaven.

"Yeah," I finally answered. "Didn't get far. Apparently she was 'hanging out with friends' at the time The Louse was murdered."

Nina snorted. "Is that what she's calling it?"

I gave her a look. "What do you mean?"

She propped her elbows on the bar revealing a vast amount of cleavage and gave me a smirk. "I believe kids these days call it 'Netflix and chill.'"

My eyes widened. "Are you telling me that the perfect Mrs. Nixon was having an affair?" Not that I blamed her, based on what I knew of her husband. Me, I'd have just divorced his ass, but not everyone had my fortitude. Or lack of patience for nonsense.

"That's what I heard."

"Do you know who with?"

She shook her head, and her long, blond hair tumbled about her shoulders. The light caught her chunky gold jewelry, making it twinkle and shine. I was always a little jealous of Nina's amazing jewelry collection. "All kinds of rumors, of course, but no one seems to actually know."

"Well, darn. I'm not sure confronting her would work, either. She's kind of a cool cucumber."

"Butter wouldn't melt," Nina agreed.

"It does give her a darn good motive for murder. And if she was with her lover instead of the friends she claimed, well, that's not a great alibi. They could have been in on it together." The wheels were churning now!

"Well, if you want a motive for murder," Nina said, perching on the stool behind the bar and casually crossing her legs, "plenty of other people had motive."

"Sure. Portia, for one. Annabelle maybe."

"Other people."

"Like whom?"

"Anyone who ever met the man, I'm betting."

A frown tugged at my lips. Enough with this beating around the bush. "Do you have someone specific in mind?" I asked.

"Barista," Lloyd all but shouted from the end of the bar. I gave him a confused look, and he dove back into his wine glass.

Nina nodded. "He's right. You know that girl who used to work at the Caffeinated Bean? She had a funny name. Delly. Dilly?" Nina tapped her long nails on the bar. "Delphi. That was it. Delphi something."

An image rose in my mind of a pixie face topped by Cookie Monster hair. "I vaguely remember her. Been a while since I've seen her, though. What happened?"

"I don't know exactly, but word on the street is The Louse got her fired, and she hasn't been able to find a job since. She had to move back home with her mother, and those two fight like cats and dogs."

"Not sure that's a motive for murder."

"You ever met her mother, you'd know it was," Lloyd piped up.

# # #

Delphi's mother lived out off Highway 30 back in the woods a good thirty minutes from town. My Camry bounced and jolted over potholes and ruts as I eased my way up the gravel road. My poor car was definitely not made for this.

At the end of the road sat a mobile home in a ghastly shade of green. How to describe it? Moldy olive, perhaps?

The front door, originally white, was spattered with mud and cracked in places. The front porch sagged as if exhausted by life in general. The siding had seen better days, pieces pulling away here and there, revealing signs of dry rot. How did fake wood rot? Of course, in the Pacific Northwest, rotting was a given, as was rust and moss.

I picked my way across the soaked lawn and winced as the steps creaked ominously beneath me. Loud and exuberant barking echoed from inside followed by a voice screaming, "Shut up, Deeks. Shut up." There were a few colorful expletives sprinkled through the shouting and barking as I rapped on the door. It flung open to reveal a young woman at least half a foot shorter than I with bright-blue hair and a heart-shaped face. Behind her, a Husky bounced up and down like he had springs on his paws, barking his head off. "Deeks, I swear. Shut. Up." Deeks ignored her.

With a heavy sigh, she turned toward me. She couldn't have been more than nineteen or twenty. A silver ring gleamed from her left nostril. "Can I help you?"

"Yes, hi. My name is Viola Roberts, and I'm assisting in the Nixon murder investigation." It wasn't a lie, exactly. I was assisting. The police just didn't know I was assisting.

The girl gave me a blank look. "What's that got to do with me?"

"You're Delphi, right?"

She nodded.

"You're the one that used to work at Caffeinated Bean, right?"

"Yeah. So?" She crossed her arms, causing the vee of her black shirt to dip slightly, and I caught a glimpse of multicolored hearts covering her bra. Cute, if you were into that "unicorns farting rainbows" sort of thing. Give me a plain black bra any day. "August Nixon is the man who got you fired."

She scowled. "Oh, that jerk. Yeah, I remember him. What happened? Somebody off him?" She didn't seem upset by the thought. Of course, that was par for the course, it seemed.

"As a matter of fact, yes."

She sniffed. "Good riddance. Man was a menace."

"Er, yes. They called him The Louse."

That got a smirk out of her. "Fits."

"May I ask what happened?"

She shrugged. "He used to come in every morning on my shift. He'd harass me, harass the other girls. A nasty piece of work, you know."

I nodded. I did know. "Go on."

"He'd complain about the coffee. It was never how he ordered it." She snorted. "Liar. He liked to watch us remake it. Like he was on a power trip or something."

Which fit what I knew of August Nixon to a tee. "But how did he get you fired?"

"One day I refused to serve him. I'd just had it, you know? Sent one of the guys to do it. Pissed him off. He went to my manager. Told him that I was coming on to him rather than the other way around. As if!" She sneered in disgust.

"I take it your manager bought the lie."

"Hook, line, and sinker." She gave an exasperated shake of her head. "Men." Her voice dripped with disgust. I wasn't sure all men deserved her disdain, but August Nixon surely did. "Anyway, my jerk of a boss fired me over it, even though The Louse was totally lying. Worse, he blackballed me around town. Nobody will hire me. Had to move back in here with my mom." She frowned at the place. "I hate it here. I'm thinking of moving to Portland. Or Seattle. Maybe I can get a job there."

I felt badly for her, but I needed more information. "So, I hate to have to ask, but where were you during the time of the murder."

Her eyes widened. "Omigosh. This is just like NCIS. I love that show!"

"Um, yeah, sure. Alibi?"

"When was he killed?" I told her, and she furrowed her brow, tapping her lower lip. The dog pushed against her legs, and she shoved him back. "Down, Deeks. Let's see. I was here. At home. As usual."

"Anyone able to vouch for that?"

"Well, mom was working and Deeks doesn't talk, so not really. But I was online like all night playing Fairy World, so there's that."

"Fairy World?"

"Yeah. You know, one of those online multiplayer games. Only with fairies instead of guys with guns."

"Sounds fun." It was also a darn good alibi. There were probably hundreds of people who could confirm it, never mind there'd be a log on her computer if someone had the savvy to find it, which I was pretty sure the police could do. "Well, obviously you're in the clear. Thanks for your time, and good luck on the job hunt."

"Thanks."

As I turned to walk down the front steps, Deeks renewed his fevered barking. Delphi slammed the door and commenced shouting at the beast.

I was no further to solving this thing than I'd been this morning. Unless you counted the discovery that Mrs. Nixon was having an affair, but without knowing who the mysterious man was, it wasn't much help.

I sighed and climbed back into the car. Tomorrow I planned to drive into Portland for Lucas's reading. Maybe he would have some ideas.

Chapter 10

"That does sound like a conundrum," Lucas admitted after I told him about Mary Nixon and her secret lover. It was Sunday afternoon, and we were sitting in The Roxy enjoying blueberry pancakes while I caught him up on all the excitement, or lack thereof.

The Roxy was the most amazing divey sort of place on Stark Street, across from Powell's Books. On the back wall was a life-sized crucifix. In the front window was a giant high-heeled shoe in leopard print. The menu items were named after famous celebrities like Dolly Parton and Steve Buscemi, and the place was frequented by drag queens. It was so totally Portland.

"It is a conundrum." I toyed with my food, oddly not as hungry as I should have been. This whole case was giving me stress. "I'm not sure how to go about confronting her."

"What would happen if you blurted it out? Hey, I know you're having an affair."

I mulled it over. "It might shock a response out of her," I said doubtfully. "But she's the most restrained person I've ever met. I mean, you met her. Nothing seems to shake her. I'm afraid she'd just turn up her nose and call the cops."

"Hmm..." He took a bite, chewing thoughtfully. He was looking particularly delicious in a cornflower-blue, button-down shirt that matched his eyes. "I suppose you could be more subtle about it. Work your way around the issue."

"Have you met me?"

He laughed. "Good point. What about a following her?"

"A stakeout?"

"Sure. The police do it, right? Maybe you can figure out who she's seeing that way."

It was a good idea, although the idea of parking in front of her house and sitting there for hours on end didn't thrill me.

"Too bad you don't know some good old-fashioned town gossips," Lucas mused, dumping cream from the baby bottle into his coffee. Yes, they served coffee creamer in baby bottles at The Roxy. All part of the charm.

My eyes widened. "But I do. Agatha, from my bunco group, is the biggest gossip you ever met. If she doesn't know something, it's not worth knowing."

"There you go then. You've got bunco tomorrow night, right?"

"Right." How did he remember that? I barely remembered half the time.

"Perfect. You can pump Agatha for information. I'm certain she'll be happy to help."

Thrilled was more like it. Nobody loved "sharing" information more than Agatha. Suddenly I wanted to jump up and drive back to Astoria, bang on Agatha's door. Instead, I smiled at Lucas. Some things are more important. Like supporting your sort-of-kind-of-boyfriend-person.

Yes, I had to find a few more ways to skin the proverbial cat, but it could wait. For now.

# # #

When I first moved to Astoria from the "big city" of Portland, I'd found myself at loose ends. With no social life to speak of, I desperately needed an outlet besides my writing. I'd joined a local yoga class. That had lasted all of five minutes, but I'd met Agatha and she'd invited me to join her bunco group. That was where I met Cheryl. The rest, as they say, was history.

The women in the bunco group greeted me cheerfully as I shoved my five dollars into an envelope and wrote my name on it. Tonight's game was at Agatha's. We took turns, each month at a different player's house. Last month it had been at Edna's, one of the founding members of the group.

"Viola. I was so sorry to hear about Portia." I was engulfed in a floral-scented hug. Cheryl's mom, Charlene, was as sweet as they came. She was a retired schoolteacher who spent her time volunteering at the Historical Preservation Society and working on various art projects.

"Thanks," I mumbled as she let me go. "It's all pretty terrible."

"That Bat." She shook her head, sending salt-and-pepper ringlets dancing. "I swear that boy needs a stern talking to. As if Portia would ever hurt anyone."

There was general agreement among the bunco ladies. Cheryl shoved a glass of wine in my hand. "You're going to need it," she murmured. "They're on a roll tonight. They're going to want every single detail of your investigation and then some."

I grinned. "And so goes bunco night."

Sure enough, as we all piled our plates with snacks and prepared to start the first round, Agatha pounced. "So, what's this I hear about an investigation?" She gave me a nudge, nudge, wink, wink motion and tucked her tongue in her cheek. Her short, gray hair was almost as spikey as Cheryl's, and she wore a flowing, Bohemian-style top with layers of beaded necklaces.

She probably knew more about it than I did at this point, but I humored her. "Well, I can't trust Detective Battersea to prove Portia's innocence," I told her as I sat at one of the card tables. "So, I figured I'd do it myself."

"I heard you did an okay job with the last investigation," she agreed, grabbing the score pad and a pen, her necklaces making a slight clicking sound as the beads hit each other. The bell rang, and Hazel, another one of our founding members, grabbed the dice and rolled. There was silence as we started our turns.

"Well, I had some help," I admitted. "But I figured if I did it once, I can do it again. I have to try. For Portia."

The other three women at the card table—Hazel, Agatha, and the quiet Rose—all nodded their heads. It was a little like receiving a benediction.

"Somebody's got to help her," Rose said softly, running fingers through her salon-golden hair. "I doubt she can afford a private detective on her salary."

I hadn't even thought of that, but Rose was right. Besides which, there wasn't' exactly an overwhelming selection of PIs in Astoria. The few that existed were mostly focused on things like cheating spouses. They'd have no idea how to properly investigate a crime. Granted, neither did I, but I'd at least seen several episodes of Lt. Joe Kenda. Not the same, I'd grant you that, but better than nothing.

As we played, I caught them up on some of the tidbits I'd found, like the lipstick. Not to mention Blaine's behavior and Mrs. Nixon's extramarital shenanigans.

"I need to question Blaine. I'm certain he's hiding something."

Agatha giggled. "Of course he is."

I stared at her. "What do you mean by that?"

"He's been dating Portia for ages. Didn't you know?"

We all shook our heads. The other two women were as keen on the news as I was. Nothing like some good gossip to perk up a game.

"Oh, yes. They were keeping it on the down-low, you know, because August Nixon would have been furious."

I frowned. "Why? Portia is an amazing person. Blaine should be so lucky."

"Exactly. Which was why August wanted her for himself, the snake. Also, I think he was hoping Blaine would marry into money so he could stop supporting the kid. Fat chance of that with Portia."

Kid? That "kid" was at least thirty years old. Maybe even thirty-five.

"Doesn't he have a job?" Hazel asked, somewhat shocked.

"Sure," Agatha said. "He's a talent rep or something, booking bands and whatnot at various venues up and down the Coast. Like that makes any money around here."

She had a point. Many coastal towns were economically depressed, completely dependent on income from tourists. "That's great info. Thanks, Agatha. I wonder why Portia didn't tell me and Cheryl. We're her friends, after all."

"Oh, you know how it is when women start dating men. They lose their ever-loving minds," Hazel said sagely.

I sighed. "Well, I guess I've got a good place to start questioning him. Now if only I could figure out who Mary Nixon was having the affair with."

"Oh, that's easy," Agatha said with a laugh.

We all stared at her. "Who?" three voices, including mine, chimed in.

"Everyone knows. Don't they?" she looked surprised.

"Spill it," Hazel snapped.

Agatha shrugged. "I thought it was common knowledge. I've seen them together several times. Twice coming out of that B&B over in Warrenton."

"Agatha!" I snarled in frustration.

"Roger Collins," she said. "Mary Nixon has been having an affair with her husband's assistant director."

□

Chapter 11

I wanted to talk to Portia first. She was supposed to be my friend, and I wanted to know more about her relationship with Blaine. And why she hadn't told me.

It took some fancy footwork, but they finally let me in to see her. When the guard ushered her into the visiting room, I couldn't hold back my astonishment. She looked nothing like the Portia I knew. Gone was the sleek sophistication and elegant fashion. She was pale, worn, with bags beneath her eyes and an equally baggy uniform in an unsightly shade of beige.

I started to hug her, but the prison guard barked, "No touching." I barely refrained from responding with a very immature tongue-sticking-out.

We sat at the Formica table in uncomfortable plastic chairs where we stared at each other for a good thirty seconds. For once, I had no idea what to say.

"Thanks for coming," Portia finally said, her fingers clasped together tightly on the table. "Sure. Of course. We're friends. It's what we do, right?"

She nodded, tears welling in her eyes. "I can't stand it in here, Viola," she whispered. "It's so awful. And this isn't even prison. If I don't get out of here—"

"It's okay," I interrupted. "I'm working on it."

She glanced at me, blue eyes wide. "How?"

"Don't worry about the how, just know I'm on the case."

"Are you sure? You could get hurt."

"This is me we're talking about."

"Yes," she said grimly. "That's what I'm worried about."

I waved airily. "I can handle myself. I've done this before."

She looked doubtful. "Thanks, I guess."

"Sure thing. Now listen, I need to ask some questions, okay?"

"Sure. What do you need to know?"

"I talked to your coworker, Annabelle. She said that you got into an argument with The Louse the day he died, and you threatened him. Is that true?"

She gave me a half-hearted smile. "It's true."

"Why didn't you tell me? If the police find out—"

"Because it's not what you think. He put his hands on me, and I snapped. Yelled at him. I told him he'd pay, but I didn't mean that I'd kill him. I meant that I was going to turn him in. Finally."

"I thought you said turning him in would do no good."

She shrugged. "Probably wouldn't. But I figured threatening him might get him to stop. At least for a while."

"Okay, I get that. One other thing." I wasn't sure how to phrase it, so I blurted it out. "I hear you're dating Blaine Nixon."

She went even paler, if that were possible. "How'd you hear that?"

"So it's true?"

She stared at her hands. "Yes." The response was so soft I barely heard her.

"Why didn't you tell me?"

She sighed. "Blaine didn't want his dad knowing about us."

"Oh, gee, that's real manly of him," I said dryly.

"It isn't like that," she insisted. "In the past, his dad has done some pretty awful things to Blaine's girlfriends."

"Like sexually harassed them?" I guessed.

"And worse, if you can imagine."

Unfortunately, I could. "What else?"

"What do you mean?"

"There has to be more to it than Blaine being afraid The Louse would come on to you. I mean, that boat already sailed, if you know what I mean."

She sighed. "I don't have the right status. His parents, especially his dad, wouldn't approve, and since he's living with them..." She shrugged.

Sounded like a major weenie to me, but I didn't want Portia feeling any worse than she already did. "Don't the Nixons have, like, a ton of money? Why do they need more? It's not like you're some kind of gold digger."

"I have no idea. All I know is that Blaine was convinced they wouldn't like us dating, and he wanted to keep it secret. At least for a while."

I thought it was idiotic, but it was Portia's life, not mine. It did seem like there was more to this than what she knew. It was time to confront Blaine.

# # #

The Dirty Dog was a pseudo-English pub down near the waterfront. It boasted the appropriate atmosphere of dark wood, gloomy lighting, and dozens of beers on tap. There was even a dartboard in one corner, although I'd never seen anyone play. The food was good, if simple, the drinks cheap(ish), and the denizens cheerful. And it was there I found one Blaine Nixon sitting at the bar, nursing something that smelled vaguely of rotten mulch. In case you missed it, I'm not a fan of beer.

"Hey, Blaine," I said, skootching onto the stool next to him. "How's it going?"

He turned bleary eyes in my direction and let out something vaguely resembling a grunt before returning to his pint.

"That good, huh? Watcha drinking?"

He ignored me.

"Yeah. Looks real appetizing. Like I can't wait to just dive in." I let out an awkward laugh. Why was this guy so hard to talk to? How on earth did I get him to open up and spill his guts?

"What'll it be?" The bartender leaned over the counter and gave me a look that told me dillydallying was frowned upon.

"Sarsaparilla. And make it strong!" I laughed awkwardly again. "Always wanted to say that."

The bartender gave me a look and braced his beefy arms on the counter. "Everyone's a comedienne. Try again."

"Heh. Okay." I squinted at the fridge behind the bar. "How about some apple juice?" I said lamely.

He shrugged and turned to grab a bottle from the fridge. A quick flick of the wrist, and the cap sailed off onto the bar top. He slid the bottle across. "Five bucks."

My eyes widened. "Are you kidding? Beer doesn't even cost that much."

"You want beer prices, you buy beer."

"Fine," I grumbled. "But I want a receipt." I dug a five-dollar bill out of my handbag and slapped it on the bar. "Receipt?"

"Coming right up."

I turned back to Blaine who'd ignored the whole altercation. "I just saw Portia."

He perked up. "You did? How is she? Is she okay?"

"She's holding up." I took a sip of my apple juice. It was nothing exciting. Certainly not worth the insane price. I was going to have to write a strongly worded letter to the manager.

"I wish there was something I could do," he said morosely.

"How about paying for a good lawyer? Getting her out of there?"

He snorted. "With what money?"

"Aren't you guys rich?"

He gave me a look. "You haven't heard?"

"Heard what?"

"The almighty August Nixon had a serious gambling problem. There's nothing left. Or not much, anyway. What little there is left went to my mom, not me."

"Oh." I wasn't sure what else to say. "Is that why you were hiding your relationship with Portia?"

"Partially. I know it sounds stupid, but both of my parents were hoping I'd marry well, you know? Prop up the family name. Which is ridiculous. Anywhere else on the planet, we're total nobodies, but in Astoria, we're Big Deals. They'd do anything to save face and keep their status intact."

"So, neither of your parents would have appreciated you dating Portia?"

"Nope."

I scowled at him. "Geez. Grow a spine, why don't you?" Sometimes I really should keep my mouth shut.

He glowered at me. "I tried. I did. But my mother was barely holding on as it was, and my father was becoming increasingly unstable."

"Like losing his mind?"

"Sort of. The gambling losses were causing a lot of stress. He snapped at the least little thing. I did not want to set him off. I figured things would settle down eventually and then I could tell them. In my own time."

"Portia seemed to think you were also trying to protect her from your father's unsavory advances."

He snorted. "As if I could do that. She worked with the guy. But it kept her off my back. At least for a while until I could figure things out." He shrugged. "Guess it doesn't matter now. Mom may be disappointed, but tough. Everyone will find out the truth about good ole August Nixon soon enough."

I mulled that over as I sucked down my bottle of juice. "So, you knew all about the money being gone."

He swallowed. "Sure."

I knew he was lying. "You had no idea! You thought you'd inherit." And that was a darn good motive for murder.

"Listen," he snapped, "I may not have known, but that didn't mean I killed the bas—my father. I had no reason to."

"How about needing money?"

"Why would I need money?" He didn't quite meet my eye. "I've got a job. Might not make me rich, but I do okay."

I wasn't so sure about that, but until I could prove otherwise, I decided to let it go. "How about an alibi?"

He rolled his eyes. "Who do you think you are? Jessica Fletcher?"

"I'm trying to help Portia. You want that, don't you?"

He sighed. "Sure. Fine. I was in Seaside at a concert."

I nodded. I would definitely check that out. "Thanks." I slid off the barstool. "I might have more questions later."

"Fine. Whatever."

I was nearly to the door when a thought struck me. "Hey, Blaine, do you know anyone called Mrs. A?"

He frowned. "You talking about that old biddy that donates to the museum?"

I stepped a little closer. "Old biddy?"

"Sure. She's been donating for years. Dad used to kiss her backside on a regular basis."

"You remember her last name?"

"Um." He rolled his eyes toward the ceiling as if it might have inspiration. "Yeah. Archer. Mrs. Glennis Archer."

I beamed at him. "Thanks!" I was out the door and nearly to my car before I realized I never got my receipt.

☐

Chapter 12

"Are you sure she has anything to do with it?" Cheryl asked, peering over my shoulder. She'd come to my place to help me investigate the mysterious Mrs. A, and now we were both sitting in my breakfast nook, staring at a picture of Glennis Archer on my laptop screen.

She was an elegant woman with her silver hair cut into a smooth bob, makeup perfectly applied, and expensive but understated jewelry. She stared back at us from a business website with an article about how she had taken over operations of the family business from her deceased husband and actually increased the company's income tenfold. That meant she was smart and savvy. Or had excellent advisers who she was intelligent enough to listen to.

"I have no idea," I admitted. "But we need to talk to her. She had an appointment with The Louse the same night he was killed. Maybe she did it."

"She doesn't look like a killer, but then they rarely do."

She made an excellent point. "Even if she didn't do it, maybe she saw who did."

Cheryl scrunched up her nose. "Any ideas how to get close to her? I doubt we could waltz into her place of business and demand to see her. They'd probably have security throw us out."

"I already tried to make an appointment. Her assistant claims she's booked for a month." Not that I believed that for a minute. "I think I need to use some finesse with her."

Cheryl gave a sort of gigglesnort.

"Hey, I can finesse when I need to."

"Yeah, well, I've got a better idea. I think we need to approach her somewhere away from her office. Somewhere she'll have her guard down and won't suspect anything."

"Like?"

"Like when she's getting her nails done or something."

"It's a good idea," I agreed. "But how are we supposed to find out when she's getting her nails done?"

"Social media, naturally." She gave me a smug look.

"You think a woman as smart and rich as Glennis Archer is going to plaster her itinerary all over the web?"

She shrugged. "Doesn't hurt to look."

I pulled up one of the most popular social media sites and did a search for Glennis Archer's name. I got a big, fat goose egg.

"Nothing. Any other ideas?"

"Try her maiden name. Maybe she's trying to keep a low profile."

Which is exactly what I would do if I were a mucky-muck like Mrs. Archer. Question was, what was her maiden name? Google searches yielded nothing. Likely she and Mr. Archer had been married years before the advent of social media. "Maybe we should ask Agatha," I suggested, only half joking. "That woman knows everything."

"Oh, good idea! Let's call her right now."

"At ten o'clock at night?"

"Sure. Apparently she doesn't sleep much."

Which might explain her propensity for gossip. Sheer boredom, no doubt. Maybe she needed a hobby besides bunco and painting. Her house was already over flowing with art.

"Agatha, hi, it's Cheryl. Mmmhmmm. Yes. Mmm. Right."

I rolled my eyes. Who knew what Agatha was going on about now? Although likely it was juicy. To somebody.

"That's so interesting," Cheryl finally blurted, "but I have a question for you."

There was excited chatter from the other end of the line. I gave Cheryl a sympathetic look.

"Actually," she said, giving me a sly look, "Viola wants to ask you herself." She shoved the phone at me and nearly doubled over in laughter.

I glared at her, but took the device. "Hi, Agatha."

"You need some information? Is it about the case?" She sounded a little too enthusiastic.

"Um, yes. It is. And we need to keep this on the down-low."

"Mum's the word," Agatha said cheerfully. "How can I help?"

"Do you know Glennis Archer?"

"Not personally," Agatha admitted, "but everyone knows Glennis Archer. I mean, her wedding was a six-day wonder."

I had no idea what that meant, but it sounded like good news. If Agatha could remember the wedding, she might remember a lot more. "Do you remember Mrs. Archer's maiden name?"

"Of course. I mean, everyone was so stunned. It was a big deal back then."

I frowned. "What was?"

"Well, the Archers were the High and Mighty, you know. Big wigs around here. Wealthy, residents for generations, that sort of thing. Fingers in every pie."

"I take it Glennis was not."

"Goodness no. She was a Clay."

"I don't know what that means," I admitted.

"The Clays were a notorious family from the wrong side of the tracks. The very wrong side, if you get my meaning."

I did. "And yet, Archer married her anyway."

"She was beautiful back then. Extremely so. And a good actress. She knew how to put on a show. Pretend to be what she wasn't. Most people have forgotten by now. Those that were around have died or moved away. Nobody remembers."

"Or cares, I imagine."

"Well, I wouldn't go that far. Glennis is a proud woman. She worked hard to create that gloss of high society. I don't think she'd be pleased if the town were reminded of where she came from."

Which could be an excellent motive for murder. "Thanks, Agatha. See you next month at bunco."

"If not sooner!"

After we said our goodbyes, I did another Internet search while catching Cheryl up on the conversation. "Here it is." I pointed to the profile. "Glennis Clay. She lists her hometown as Rock Beach."

Cheryl made a face like she'd smelled rancid fish. "Are you kidding me?"

"Why? It's a decent place. Nice beach. Good cafes."

"It is now, but ten years ago that place was a dump. One of the worst towns on the northern coast. There were a few rundown houses, a dodgy bar, and that was pretty much it. The residents spent most of the time drunk. Locals avoided the place like the plague."

"And Glennis came from that?"

"Yep. It was only about a decade ago that tourists discovered the beach and started buying up plots of land for weekend getaways. The town changed practically overnight." Cheryl nodded at the profile picture of Glennis Clay Archer looking sassy in a red and white striped sweater with perfectly coiffed hair. "Amazing. You'd never know it looking at her." She certainly didn't look like someone who came from the place Cheryl described.

I scrolled through Glennis's profile, trying to find something, anything that would give me a clue as to where we could track her down. Then I found it. She'd liked the page of a bar in a nearby town called Winos and Riffraff.

"That sounds promising," Cheryl said with a giggle. "Talk about truth in advertising."

"Well, we can't just show up there and hope for the best. Even if she goes there—which it doesn't seem like her kind of place—we have no idea when she goes there.
"

Cheryl sighed. "Good point. Does that mean we're back to a stake-out?"

"Looks like."

#

In books and movies, they always talked about how stakeouts weren't fun. How they were boring, tedious, and so on. Well, they were actually worse than you could possibly imagine.

Cheryl and I decided to stake out Glennis Archer's house Friday evening. We figured that if she went out that night, she'd have to come home first to change or whatever. So, about four o'clock we pulled up and parked across the street a few doors down. And waited. And waited.

An hour in, I had to pee.

"Can't you hold it?" Cheryl asked.

"You know I can't. I've got a bladder the size of a peanut."

Cheryl rolled her eyes. "I should have kept you from drinking that last cup of coffee."

"I needed it to stay awake."

"Why don't you pee in the empty coffee cup?"

I stared at her. "Are you serious? No way. Gross."

"Well, I don't know what you're going to do, then. We can't leave or we might miss her. And you can't go in the bushes. It's broad daylight in the middle of an upscale neighborhood. You'll get arrested."

She was right about that. Glennis Archer lived at the top of the hill almost to the Column in an enormous, rambling, pristine white house with a lawn that had been manicured within an inch of its life. It was not the sort of place where you squatted behind a bush.

"Fine. We're like twenty blocks from Commercial Street. There are plenty of shops and whatnot still open. I'm sure I can find a place that will let me in. I'm going to need the car, though."

She sighed. "And what am I supposed to do while you're gone?"

"Up the hill a little way is a pull out. You can still see the house from there, but you can pretend you're resting from a hike or something."

She rolled her eyes. "Well, hurry up. We don't want to miss her because you're off messing around."

"Text me if she gets home." With that, I pulled out down the hill toward Commercial Street, Astoria's main drag. Fortunately, the first cafe I came to knew me well and let me use their facilities. Out of gratitude, I bought two muffins and headed back up the hill. I pulled the car into place, and Cheryl climbed in.

"Better?" she asked.

"Much," I said, tossing her one of the muffins.

"Blueberry. My fave. Thanks."

"No problem." I'd kept the chocolate for myself, naturally. "Anything?"

"Not a thing. No sign of Mrs. Archer or anyone else, for that matter." She eyed my outfit. "You know, I don't understand why you wore all black."

"To better blend in, of course."

She stared at me, her mouth full of muffin. "You do know it's the middle of the day, don't you?"

A tapping at the window startled us out of our wits. Cheryl dropped her muffin. I had a mini heart attack.

Outside the car stood a diminutive woman that looked about a thousand years old. She was wearing a blue and white housedress and had pink curlers in her hair. I could see pale scalp shining through the thin strands wrapped around the rollers. I rolled down the window.

"Hello?" I gave her a cheery smile.

"You girls lost?" Her voice had a querulous quality to it.

"Um, why do you ask?"

"You been sitting in front of my house for an hour and a half. Then you ran off, and I figured you were gone. Then you come back. Are you casing the joint or something?"

Oh, great, a Nosey Parker. Just our luck. "Well, no, we're waiting for someone, actually." I winced a little, but I figured by the time Nosey Parker was able to spill the beans to Mrs. Archer, we'd have already confronted her.

"Is that so?" The woman crossed her arms over her scrawny bosom. "Who would you be waiting for?"

"Mrs. Archer," I said, cool as a cucumber.

The old woman snickered. "You're gonna be waiting a while then, dearie."

"Why is that?"

She gave me a doubtful look. "Well, I don't know as I should be telling a stranger."

"But I'm not a stranger," I soothed. "My name is Viola Roberts, and I'm a friend of Mrs. Archer's." Which was a total lie, but how was the old lady to know?

She gave me a long measuring look. "I don't know..."

"Oh, please." Cheryl leaned over and gave her big, brown eyes. "We've come a long way to see her."

The old woman squinted at Cheryl. "Huh. Well, as you're friends, I guess it's all right." She leaned closer to the car. "Thing is, the Archer woman never comes home on Friday nights. Out until the wee hours of Saturday she is, and dressed like a hussy." She looked like she was sucking on lemons. "Not that I'm one to judge." Ha! "But it doesn't seem fitting, a woman like her dressing and behaving like that. Been that way since her husband died. God rest his soul."

Cheryl and I exchanged glances. "Well, then, I guess we'll come back tomorrow," I said.

"You do that."

"Thank you," I called as I started the car and pulled out onto the road.

"Where are we headed?" Cheryl asked.

"We just got our answer." I grinned. "Winos and Riffraff, here we come."

Shéa MacLeod

Chapter 13

Winos and Riffraff turned out to be a classic, beach-town dive bar. The ramshackle building was sagging and weather worn, huddled off the side of Highway 101 all by its lonesome, surrounded by a large, gravel parking lot filled with rusted pickups and cars with multicolored door panels.

The minute I opened the door, the din hit me. The screech of the dying sound system almost drowned out the band and people trying to shout over the top of each other. It was dim, lit in an eerie, bluish lighting that made everyone look like zombies. Cheryl made a face and stuck her fingers in her ears. I couldn't blame her. The noise level was deafening. Even worse was the stench of stale beer and, under that, the faintest odor of vomit and backed-up sewer lines. I desperately wanted to turn around and walk out, but we had a job to do.

I stood just inside the door and scanned the crowd for Mrs. Archer, but I couldn't see a classy, silver-haired lady anywhere. Mostly it was locals in flannel, fleece, and worn jeans, leather-clad bikers on a road trip, or overdressed tourists from Portland. I definitely had a hard time picturing Glennis Archer in a place like this. Glennis Clay, on the other hand...

A local band was on the stage playing a bizarre cross of country and hip-hop that made my ears bleed. They played loudly and enthusiastically, but not terribly well. A few brave souls littered the dance floor, swaying to the heavy beat, but most of the patrons huddled around the bar, booths along the back wall, or the small round tables taking up most of the floor. They were far more interested in their beer than in the music.

I sauntered toward the bar, my feet sticking to the floor as I walked. I didn't even want to think about what was living on that floor. Cheryl followed close behind. She looked nervous. I hoped I didn't look as nervous. A place like this you could get eaten alive. I swaggered to the nearest empty barstool and hoisted myself onto it, nearly toppled off, righted myself, and gave the hunky bartender a sexy grin and a hair flip. He stared me down, unimpressed. Clearly he had no taste.

Cheryl perched on the stool next to me with a great deal more grace. The bartender eyed her with interest. Figured. But maybe she'd get a date out of this. That would be something. The girl was still mooning over Max What's-his-name. They'd really hit it off in Florida, but the minute the conference was over, he was on his merry way. Men.

"What'll it be?" the bartender shouted over the raucous.

"Blackberry bourbon. On the rocks." I shouted back. He didn't even look at me.

"I'll have a martini." Cheryl gave him a big smile.

"Sure thing, little lady."

Her smile turned to a scowl as he turned to make our drinks. "Did he just call me—"

"Yep. He sure did." I could practically see the steam rolling out her ears.

"Why, that..." She half stood from her stool.

I grabbed her and pulled her back down. "Hey, at least let him make us our drinks before you punch his lights out."

She sat down, clearly still fuming. She mumbled something which I couldn't hear. Probably for the best.

The bartender returned with our drinks. He gave Cheryl a long, slow look. I think it was supposed to be sexy. I could tell she was trying not to strangle him.

"You have fun," I said, sliding off my stool. "I'm going to mingle. See if I can spot Glennis."

Cheryl opened her mouth, probably to argue, but I squeezed between a couple of dancers and hurried away before she could say anything. No doubt I'd get an earful for abandoning her, but we were on the job here.

I strolled around the edge of the dance floor, carefully eyeing each patron. I saw no one who resembled Glennis Archer. Maybe the nosey neighbor was wrong. Maybe Mrs. Archer wasn't at the Wino. Maybe she was at some other club or bar in some other town.

And then I spotted silver hair. I stopped dead, stunned. The woman was clearly Glennis Archer, but she looked nothing like her photo. Instead of sleek hair, understated makeup, and an expensive suit, her hair had been spiked up with gel. She had more makeup on than one of those TV evangelist women, and she was wearing black leather pants and a sequined top, of all things. But what really caught my eye was the particularly bright shade of pink lipstick.

Gotcha!

I pulled out my phone to text Cheryl, but had no signal. What kind of bar had no cell service? I started back to the bar to grab her when I tripped over someone's massive, booted foot.

"Hey, little lady," a voice boomed in my ear. What was with that phrase tonight? "Sorry, about that." A beefy hand wrapped around my upper arm and held on a little too long. I tried to pull away, but he wouldn't let go.

"Hey—" I started, then stopped. The man was massive. Probably six foot seven and solid muscle except for a slight paunch around the middle. He had a black bandana tied around his head and a big, bushy, red beard that probably hid a week's worth of food. I forced down my gag reflex. I'd never been one for beards. "No problem," I choked out, trying to subtly free myself from the beefy man. He didn't let go. "Could I please have my arm back?"

"Well, now, I'm thinking not. I'm thinking you should join me and my buddies for a drink." Beefy gestured to a table full of leering men wearing way too much leather and not nearly enough deodorant.

I threw back my shoulders, which had the unfortunate effect of drawing attention to my ample bosom. "I'm only going to say this once." Anyone who knew me would know that tone of voice meant danger. "Get your hand off me."

"Oh, come on," Beefy said, propping himself on the edge of a table with one hand while still holding on to me with the other. "Be a sport." He and his compatriots leered at me.

I sighed. "Fine. You asked for it." I snagged a fork off the nearest table and stabbed it full force into Beefy's hand. He let out a howl and dropped me like a hot potato.

"Why you little—" He swung. I ducked. His fist planted into the back of the head of a man who'd been standing behind me. The man's beer sprayed all over half the dance floor. He swung around and, without so much as a word, punched Beefy in the face.

Next thing I knew, there was a full-on brawl. I could see Cheryl's terrified face at the bar. I waved to her and pointed at the retreating back of Glennis Archer. I knew the minute Cheryl recognized her. Cheryl gave me a thumbs-up and slipped out of the bar after Mrs. Archer.

Meanwhile, things were getting precarious. Someone had picked up a chair and slammed it over someone else's head. Unfortunately, the chair was metal, so there was quite a lot of blood. Some of it hit my shoe. Ew.

I tiptoed around the mess, trying to wend my way through the teaming crowd without getting any more involved than I already was. A fist flew my direction, and I dodged to the right, stepping on someone's foot. The foot kicked out, but I darted to the left, narrowly avoiding it. It connected with someone else, and the brawl spread.

By the time I made it to the door, the music had finally stopped and the bartender was shouting into a cell phone. Probably to the police. How did he have cell reception in here? I slipped out the door and into the dimly lit parking lot and let out a massive sigh of relief.

Scanning the lot, I caught sight of Cheryl standing next to a snazzy little roadster, arguing with the occupant. I strode over, ready for battle.

"You can't leave," Cheryl was saying.

"I most certainly can, young woman. Now move out of my way or I'll run you over." The imperious tone could only belong to our quarry.

"Glennis Clay Archer, I presume?" I said, leaning up against the side of the car and poking my head through the passenger window.

She turned to stare at me. "Who on earth are you?"

I reached in, unlocked the door, and slid into the passenger seat. It was surprisingly comfy. "Viola Roberts."

"What are you doing in my car? Get out or I'll—"

"You'll what? Call the cops? Have your face plastered all over the morning paper? I don't think so."

Her expression grew tight, face pale. "What do you want?"

"I've got a few questions for you. No biggie."

Her jaw muscle flexed. "I can't stay here. I need to leave before the authorities arrive."

She was keeping her posh tone, but her outfit was total white trash. "That's fine. I'll ride along with you while Cheryl follows."

Glennis opened her mouth to protest, but I gave her a look.

"This is highly irregular," she muttered.

"So is murder."

"Murder?" she screeched. "You're going to murder me?"

"Don't be an idiot," I snapped. "I'm a writer, not a killer. I'm talking about The Louse."

She blinked, confused. "Who?"

"August Nixon."

"Oh, him." She rolled her eyes. "I should have known. The Louse is an accurate name for him. There's a diner down the road. Will that do?"

"Works for me."

# # #

"You have to understand, I can't have this getting out." Glennis kept her voice low, head tilted away from the rest of the diner so that her hair hid half her face. "I have a certain reputation to uphold. My business depends on it."

"Mrs. Archer—" I broke off as the waitress appeared to take our orders.

Makin' Bacon was a cleverly named fifties-style diner on the east side of Highway 101, halfway between Winos and Astoria. It would have had a great view of the ocean if the other side of the highway hadn't been a veritable forest of fir trees. Outside it was windy, cold, and rainy, turning the muddy parking area into a thick soup. Inside it was toasty warm, steaming up the windows until you couldn't make out anything but a vague glow from the outside lights.

The floor was a classic black-and-white checkerboard, though the white had been scuffed enough to turn it grayish. The walls were mint green to match the faux leather booths. The white Formica tables matched the counter. The glass dessert display was filled with every kind of pie you could possibly imagine from classic marionberry to Southern-style sweet-potato merengue. Behind the counter was an old-fashioned milkshake machine that was clearly still in use. The air was perfumed with a myriad of scents from maple syrup and pancakes to fried chicken with an undertone of burned coffee and dried ketchup.

The waitress poured our requested cups of coffee, confirmed that we wanted nothing else, and sauntered away, her strawberry-blond ponytail swinging cheerfully. I made sure she was far enough from the table before continuing the conversation.

"Listen, we don't want to out you or anything, but we have some important questions for you about August Nixon."

"Fine." She took a delicate sip of coffee, every inch the lady of the manor despite her appearance. "Ask away."

I nodded and sipped my own coffee before nearly spitting it out. In a state known for its coffee obsession, some restaurants sure hadn't got the memo. I subtly pushed the mug away. No way was I drinking that swill. Maybe I'd have pie instead. The cardamom rhubarb with bourbon crust looked tasty.

"The night of the murder, I noticed two empty wine glasses on Mr. Nixon's desk. One of them had lipstick on it. A very particular shade of lipstick." I gave her mouth a pointed look. She touched her lower lip self-consciously. "In addition, there was an appointment noted in his calendar with a Mrs. A. His son confirmed that you, Mrs. Archer, are a patron of the museum and frequently met with Mr. Nixon."

"Fine. It was me. I met with August at seven o'clock the night he died. But he was very much alive when I left."

"When was that?" Cheryl asked. She'd pulled out a notebook from goodness knew where and was jotting down notes. I'd turn her into a proper investigator yet.

"Just after seven thirty. I had a dinner appointment at eight and didn't want to miss it."

"Half an hour. That's not very long for a glass of wine," I mused.

She gave an aggravated sigh. "The truth is, I barely touched my wine. If the glass was empty, August likely finished it off. I was too upset to drink."

I lifted an eyebrow. "Do tell."

She stiffened. "I don't think it's any of your business."

"No," I agreed. "But then neither is the fact you like to spend Friday nights in a low-class joint like the Wino, but I do happen to know about it." There may or may not have been a slight edge of warning in my tone. Would I really rat her out? Probably not, but she didn't know that, and I wasn't above making threats if it meant saving my friend.

Glennis ground her teeth. "Fine," she spat. "If you must know, I was there to inform August that I could no longer function as patron of the Flavel House. I was withdrawing my financial support."

"Why?" Cheryl blurted, eyes wide. "It must be an amazing tax write-off." Trust Cheryl to be practical about such things.

"It is," Glennis admitted. "But lately..." She swallowed, her fingers strumming nervously on the table, though she seemed unaware of it. "Lately things have taken a bit of a downturn. The company is struggling. It's temporary, but I need to put money into the business. Besides which, I'd heard some...unsavory rumors."

"Unsavory rumors? About August Nixon?" There may have been a slight bit of sarcasm in my tone.

"Yes." She stared into her mug. "You must understand, I have no proof of this, but if what I heard is true...well, it doesn't look good at all."

"What?" Cheryl and I blurted out.

"I assume by now you know of August's gambling debts?"

We both nodded.

"According to my sources, he was in a bind to pay those debts quickly and quietly...or else." She drew a finger across her throat. "You get my meaning."

We did.

"August Nixon has been stealing from the museum for months."

☐ **Chapter 14**

"Good grief." Nina paused in the middle of organizing one of her wine displays to stare at me. After we'd parted ways with Mrs. Archer, Cheryl and I headed straight to Sip. "How on earth did he think he could get away with it?"

"That's the million-dollar question," I agreed. "Glennis Archer didn't know the details, so I desperately need to talk to Roger Collins now. Surely he knows something." I had promised Glennis that I wouldn't get her involved or let anyone know where Cheryl and I had found her, but to my mind, that didn't include Nina. Naturally, I told her everything.

"That would explain a lot," Nina admitted as she placed a final bottle on the shelf and folded up her stepladder.

"What do you mean?" Cheryl asked before I could.

"People are funny. They're creatures of habit. And when it comes to wine, those habits are usually formed not only by their taste buds, but by their finances and perceptions."

"Okay, I get the first two. But perceptions?" I asked.

She set a bottle of wine on the bar. It was a lovely pinot noir with a twenty-dollar label. I knew for a fact it was delicious, with flavors of vanilla, pomegranate, and berries. I didn't prefer the mineral taste, but that was a light undertone, barely noticeable.

"This is a good wine," Nina said. "Solid. Not too pricey. In fact, it's one of the better pinots I sell. Now you, Viola, are a woman with a solid palate who doesn't give a rip what anyone thinks of you. You can afford more expensive wine if you want to, but you don't feel the need to throw away good money when this affordable wine is so much better than something twice the price."

I grinned. "You nailed me in one."

She set two more bottles of pinot noir on the counter. One was half the price, and one was nearly double. "These bottles are also decent."

"Because you don't carry a bad wine," Cheryl said confidently.

Nina nodded graciously. "I try. The point is, pinot noir drinkers on a budget would go for this one." She touched the neck of the cheaper bottle. "It's not as good as the first wine, but it is good and it fits the budget conscious."

A.k.a, the broke.

"The more expensive bottle is actually no better than the twenty-dollar bottle. It's good, of course, but there's no need to pay extra when the other wine is just as good. However, there is a certain prestige to being able to toss enough cash to drink a bottle of thirty-eight-dollar wine when everyone else is drinking the twenty."

"What does this have to do with The Louse?" Cheryl asked.

Nina carefully put the wines away. "August Nixon has always been a thirty-eight-dollar drinker. He cared far more about appearances than quality or taste. About a year ago, however, he dropped to ten-dollar wine for about six months or so. Then suddenly he was back to the more expensive stuff. I assumed, you know, he'd gone through a rough patch and that he'd recovered. It happens."

"Now you're thinking his financial upswing coincides with the museum thefts," I guessed.

She nodded. "That was my thought, yes."

"Do you remember when exactly that happened?"

She stared at the ceiling for a moment, trying to recall. "Last summer is when he dropped to the cheap stuff. Three months ago, he went back to his old habits."

"Thanks," I said. "Tomorrow I'll see if Roger can corroborate."

# # #

Roger Collins wasn't exactly what I expected. Not that August Nixon had been a prize, but I had figured that Mary Nixon would've had more exacting taste the second time around. Maybe even a younger man.

In fact, Roger Collins was nearly a decade older than August Nixon and probably should have been retired years ago. He wore his white hair longish down the back, but carefully tucked into an orderly queue, and a neatly trimmed goatee, also pure white. He was like an aging hippie who hadn't quite caught on to the rest of the world yet. I was horrified to find he wore socks with his sandals. My nose was equally horrified to discover he was overly fond of patchouli. If Mary was aiming for the opposite of August, she'd done it.

"Won't you come into my office?" he asked, ushering me up the stairs of the Flavel carriage house in a gentlemanly fashion. He had a slight drawl that was impossible to place. "Would you like a cup of tea? I'm certain we have some around here somewhere." He paused looked around vaguely as if tea would suddenly appear in the middle of the stairwell.

"We're out, Mr. C," Annabelle chirped from her position at the register. It was apparently her turn in the gift shop today. "I can go grab some at the coffee shop, if you want?"

"No, thanks. I'm fine." I assured them both.

Satisfied that I wasn't about to expire with thirst, Roger continued up the stairs with me following close behind. The carriage house sat at the edge of the Flavel property and had been converted into a combination gift shop/ticket box on the main floor with offices and a small employee lounge on the top floor.

We passed a closed door with a large sign declaring "August Nixon, Director." A plan formed in my brain, but I shoved it aside. For now.

Halfway down the short hall, Roger swung open a door with a sign that read "R. Collins - Asst. Dir." I wondered if they had to pay per letter.

His office suited him to a tee. It was like something straight out of a movie. The high-ceilinged room boasted a small, cast-iron chandelier and rustic wall sconces. Shelves of books and knickknacks took up every available wall. Heavy curtains turned the room almost gloomy. Heavy Victorian furniture and a wine-red carpet added to the gloom. The large oak desk was piled high with stacks of books and files which leaned precariously toward the edge, threatening to leap off at any moment and make a run for it.

Roger hurriedly cleaned off a straight-backed chair and urged me to sit while he climbed over a stack of encyclopedias to get to his own chair behind the desk. It creaked heavily as he sank into it. He let out a heartfelt sigh. "Now, how may I assist you, Miss…Violet, was it?"

"Viola," I corrected.

"What a lovely name. Were you named after the flower? Or the instrument?"

"My great-grandmother."

"Ah." He nodded sagely as if that explained everything.

"I'm here because I'm helping the police with their investigations into Mr. Nixon's murder," I said. It was a bit of a lie. Bat would no doubt be furious if he found out I was claiming to be working with the police, but who would tell him?

"Nasty business, that," Roger said, expression grim. He glanced around, dug under some papers, and came out with a plastic bag of gummy bears. "Something sweet?" he offered.

"No thanks." With my luck, they were pot gummies. Totally legal now, but still not my thing.

He shrugged. "Suit yourself." He popped one into his mouth and chewed lazily. "How are you helping, exactly?"

He was sharper than he seemed. Not such a hippie pothead after all. "Just talking to people. Tying up loose ends. That sort of thing."

"How odd."

"They're short staffed."

"Well, anything I can do to help." He folded his hands neatly on the desk. "August was not my favorite person, but his family did not deserve to be put through that kind of loss."

"Did you know about Mr. Nixon's gambling problem?"

He stilled. "Unfortunately, yes." His tone hinted at extreme displeasure.

"So, you knew he was stealing from the museum."

He took a moment to answer and finally let out a sigh. "Yes. I caught him at it."

"And he was okay with that?" I couldn't imagine August would be pleased that his underling could hold something like that over him.

"Not really," he said grimly. "He threatened to frame me for it if I told anyone."

"Sounds like an excellent motive for murder."

"It would be," he admitted. "Except I have an alibi." He popped another gummy.

"And it is...?"

"Oh, yes. I was at a pot party." He chewed enthusiastically.

Of course he was. "Of course you were. What's a pot party?"

"It's like a potluck, but everyone brings pot to share. Edibles, smokes, whatever."

"That's a thing?"

"Sure. Has been since the sixties. Only it's legal now. Police already confirmed my alibi."

Well, there went a great suspect. Darn it. "Out of curiosity, what exactly was he doing? And how did he pull it off? August, I mean."

"Well..." He chewed thoughtfully. "Like most museums, Flavel House has many items that have been donated throughout the years. Most of them aren't even on display. It's easy enough to liberate one or two items from storage and sell them on eBay. I'm afraid security around here is fairly lax. And this is a small-town museum with a small team. Mostly volunteers. Normally it would be years before the theft was discovered, if ever. So, it was fairly easy. Apparently he'd been doing it for months. A vase here. A first edition there."

"Do you know when he started?"

"Not precisely, no. But from what I can extrapolate, for at least the last three or four months."

Which jibed with Nina's observation that August had been able to afford more expensive wine again three months ago. I was surprised, knowing what I did of his lack of moral compass, that it had taken August that long to come up with the idea of stealing the museum's artifacts.

"One other thing, Mr. Collins."

"Roger, please."

Was it just me or were his eyes getting glassy? "Roger. Rumor has it that you were having an affair with August Nixon's wife."

"Mary? Oh, yes. For the last two or three years. But it's all over now." He gave a long sigh, his face turning into a sad, hangdog expression. "I miss her." He popped two more gummies. "You have no idea."

Since I'd never had an affair with anyone's wife, I supposed he was right about that. I gave him what I hoped was a sympathetic smile. "When did you end it?"

"Oh, I didn't. She did. About a month ago."

Which was interesting, since Mary Nixon had claimed they were still an item.

☐

Chapter 15

My phone vibrated in my pocket as I parked my car a few blocks away from Flavel House. I pulled it out and glared at the screen glowing in the dark. It was nearly ten at night. I totally forgot that he'd promised to call. "Hello, Lucas."

"You sound put out."

Oops. I guess my impatience was showing. "Oh, no, I'm just, ah, busy. Distracted."

"Busy? Are you writing?"

I didn't think lying to Lucas was a good idea, but no way could I tell him the truth. He'd lecture me for sure. "More like research."

There was a lengthy pause. "Are you snooping, Viola?"

"Why would you assume that?" I tried to sound offended, but it was difficult when he'd hit the hammer on the nail so thoroughly.

"Maybe because it seems to be your favorite pastime these days. What are you up to this time?"

I sighed. "I can't tell you."

I could almost see him pinching the bridge of his nose. "You're breaking and entering again, aren't you?"

"I have no idea what you're talking about."

"Just be careful, okay? Try not to get arrested. Or murdered."

I laughed. "Everything is fine. Stop worrying. I've gotta go."

He mumbled something about "worrying comes with the job description" before bidding me goodnight and hanging up. I shook my head as I stuffed my phone back in my pocket and climbed out of the car. The Flavel House loomed above me, a dark, spooky presence against the night sky. Everyone had long gone home, and the only light was the soft amber glow of the front porchlight.

I double-checked my kit. Which was technically my cross-body purse. Gloves for preventing fingerprints? Check. Screwdriver for jimmying locked desk drawers? Check. Full charge on phone for photo evidence and flashlight? Check. Excuse for being in the carriage house long after closing? Well, I'd figure that one out on the fly.

I quickly walked the few blocks to the museum and skirted around to the carriage house. I paused at the bottom of the steps leading to the main floor. It was one of those things where the sloping hill created an almost daylight basement effect with the bottom half of the basement exposed rather than underground. I'd noticed on my earlier visit that there were two doors into the basement. One a restroom for visitors and the other marked "private." I was hoping the "private" door was connect to the main floor somehow.

The lock was flimsy, and I made short work of it with help from a mini bolt cutter—why I had purchased the thing, I didn't know, but it seemed a good idea at the time.

I pushed the door open and stepped inside before shutting it carefully behind me. Using my phone's flashlight app, I scanned the basement. Sure enough, there were steps leading upward to another door.

Bingo!

The door was unsurprisingly locked, but it was one of those little knob locks that anyone over the age of five can unlock with a screwdriver. And I just happened to have a screwdriver.

Standing still in the gift shop, I tried to orient myself in the dark. The Louse's office was upstairs on the right. I winced as the stairs creaked heavily under my feet. Not that it mattered. Nobody there but me and the ghosts. Not that I believed in ghosts, mind you, but it was certainly spooky enough.

The Louse's office was also locked, but again, I made short work of it. Honestly, they needed to invest in better locks. Not that it would have made a difference since the employees were doing the stealing.

I shone my flashlight around, revealing an office even more luxurious than Roger's. A plush, red couch sat along one wall with an expensive-looking oil painting hanging above it. The chandelier was crystal, and the wall sconces much more elegant than Roger's. The books in here were expensive, leather-bound tomes that had never been touched instead of the cheap, heavily thumbed paperbacks in Roger's office, and the desk looked like something appropriate for a man with a Napoleon complex.

I figured the place to start was the desk, so I pulled open the first drawer and immediately made a face. Sure, there was the usual tape, stapler, extra pens, and whatnot, but there were also several foil-wrapped prophylactics and a large tube of lube. Gross. August Nixon was a bigger louse than I thought. His poor wife.

The second drawer contained neatly labeled manila envelopes full of receipts, a flashlight with extra batteries, and a first aid kit. How practical. I pulled out some of the receipts, but there was nothing interesting. Mostly gas station fill-ups, business lunches, and the occasional stop for stationary supplies. There was certainly nothing to indicate how August Nixon had been robbing the museum blind.

The final drawer was locked. Voila!

Digging around in my purse, I brought out the yellow-handled screwdriver. It was one of those flat blade ones, perfect for jimmying open drawers. About five minutes, a lot of cussing, and several gouges into the wood later (which I felt rather guilty about), I managed to pop open the third drawer. I gave a sigh of disappointment. There was nothing there but more files.

I pulled them out one at a time. One held research notes on possible future patrons. Easy to understand why he'd lock up such sensitive information. Another held personal bank records. Probably trying to hide the true nature of their finances from his wife. Or maybe he just liked to have an extra set away from the house, in case the place burned down or something. That was writer's brain for you. I could come up with all kinds of interesting scenarios.

I dug through the files until I hit the bottom of the drawer. Nothing. Now what?

I dumped the files back in the drawer and frowned as something struck me as odd. I stared at the drawer trying to figure out what it was. Then I realized. The inside of the drawer wasn't quite as deep as it should be.

Pulling the files back out, I dumped them on the desk and knelt in front of the drawer. I pressed the bottom of the drawer gently. There was a bit of give. I wanted to cheer out loud, but that didn't really jibe with this clandestine excursion, so I bit my tongue and felt along the edges of the drawer bottom. Sure enough, there was a little depression along the back. I pressed down, and the front of the drawer bottom popped up, revealing a secret compartment beneath the false bottom.

Inside was a little, navy blue, leather-bound notebook. A red ribbon marked a page near the middle. I snagged the notebook, letting the false bottom fall back into place. After replacing the files in the drawer and closing it, I turned my attention to my new find.

I grinned like a Cheshire cat as I flipped to the marked page. I had all the evidence I needed. How it would prove Portia's innocence, I had no idea, but I needed to get this to Detective Battersea straight away.

Standing up, I started toward the door when a shock of pain lanced my skull. The floor rushed up to meet me a split second before everything went dark.

☐

Chapter 16

"Ms. Roberts? Viola? Can you hear me?"

I swam slowly to the surface, consciousness taking over. I wished it hadn't. My head throbbed like a marching band had taken up residence, and my stomach was a fraction of an inch from rebelling all over the carpet that my face was currently smooshed into.

I swallowed and turned my head slightly. My tongue felt thick. "Wh—what happened?" I squinted as the man's face zoomed in and out of focus.

"You've had a bit of an accident, Ms. Roberts," the man said. He had on a white shirt with some kind of patch on it. And was that a stethoscope around his neck? "We should get her to the hospital." He turned to someone else standing behind him.

The "someone else" moved, and I recognized Detective Battersea's forbidding expression. "I need to question her." Oh, that wasn't good.

"And you can," said the man in the white shirt, "after a doctor's looked her over. She's likely got a concussion. Possibly a serious one."

Bat grimaced. "Fine. But I'll be visiting her at the hospital."

I tried to drum up some irritation that they were talking about me like I was a non-entity, but I couldn't manage. My head hurt too badly.

The man in the white shirt, along with a woman in similar clothing, loaded me onto a gurney. EMTs. They had to be. I still couldn't figure out what was going on. An accident? What accident? And why was the detective there?

As they hauled me out on the gurney, I realized I was at the Flavel carriage house. It all came flooding back to me: the breaking and entering, snooping around The Louse's desk, finding the notebook, and then getting hit on the head. I patted myself down, finding no sign of my discovery.

"The notebook!"

"Take it easy Ms. Roberts," the woman shushed me. "You need to rest."

"What notebook?" Bat leaned over me, looking grim.

I swallowed. "I found a notebook. It totally proved August Nixon was stealing from the museum. I was going to bring it to you."

"Where is it now?"

"I don't know. Probably whoever hit me on the head has it."

He gave a deep sigh. "Ms. Roberts, you are a pain in my backside. I'll see you at the hospital."

# # #

"You're lucky Roger Collins has decided not to press charges for breaking and entering," Detective Battersea said sternly as he perched on the chair next to my hospital bed.

"I didn't break," I said stubbornly. He gave me a look. "Okay, I did break, but it was necessary."

He rolled his eyes. "Of course it was."

I'd spent the last couple of hours being poked, prodded, and scanned half to death. The doctor determined that I had a concussion and would be fine, but he wanted me in the hospital overnight "for observation." Which was annoying. The hospital bed was ridiculously uncomfortable, and nurses arrived every five minutes to take my blood pressure and assure themselves I wasn't dead. How anyone could get any rest was beyond me.

"Have you found the notebook?" I asked, ignoring the detective's snarky attitude. Not that I blamed him. Much. What I'd done was sort of illegal, and I really could be a pain in the backside. Ask my mother. I'd been annoying her for more than forty years.

"Not a trace of it."

"That means the person who hit me over the head and took it must be the killer."

He pressed his fore and middle fingers of each hand to his temples as if his head ached. "That is speculation, Viola. It could have been anyone who took it."

"But why would 'anyone' take the notebook unless it implicated them?"

"A lot of reasons," he said with exasperation.

"But after the threat..." I bit my tongue.

One eyebrow went up. "What threat?" he bit out.

"Um, well, the other day I was at Roger Collins's house. I wanted to ask him some questions." Bat rolled his eyes, and I ignored him. "He wasn't home, but when I got back to the car, there was a note on it."

"I don't suppose you still have the note." His tone was dry.

"Of course I do. I'm not an idiot. Hand me my purse, will you?" He did, and I dug around in my wallet until I found the note. I handed it to him with an air of triumph.

Bat looked over the note and gave an exasperated sigh. "Why didn't you tell me about this? This is serious."

"I realize that. I'm telling you now."

He tucked the note inside an evidence bag. "I'll have to turn this in. We'll do what we can to find out who wrote it, but it's unlikely we'll find anything."

"Fine. Whatever. What do you want to bet the person who put that note on my car is the same person who hit me on the head and stole the journal?"

"It's impossible to say," he said. "Do you recall anything that was in the journal?"

I dredged up a memory of the few pages I'd seen. "He kept detailed records from what I could tell. Names and descriptions of the artifacts along with their value, who he'd sold them to, and for how much. That sort of thing. Also how he'd covered up the theft. Faked paperwork mostly, from what I could tell."

"You remember any of the items or names?"

I rubbed the side of my nose, trying to remember details that were more than a little fuzzy. "I remember that one of the items was a statuette. It had some kind of number alongside the description. Like a serial number or something. He sold it for two hundred fifty dollars, I think."

Bat leaned back and crossed his ankles. "Any idea who the buyer was?"

I shook my head and winced as pain knifed through my skull. "Ouch. Um, no. Those were in some kind of code, from what it looked like. I'm guessing there was a key somewhere, but if there was, I didn't see it."

"Or it was in Nixon's head."

"Or that," I agreed, pulling the blanket up a little higher. I felt vaguely uncomfortable lying around in skimpy hospital garb in front of Bat, despite the fact he didn't seem to notice.

"You remember the code?"

I scrunched up my forehead, trying to remember the string of letters and numbers. "I don't remember the entire code, but the first three letters were WTF."

He gave me a look. "You're kidding."

"I am not," I assured him. "It's why I can remember."

"Any idea who that is?"

"None at all. You could ask Roger Collins."

He nodded and scribbled in his notebook.

"Or Annabelle."

He glanced up. "The girl in the gift shop?"

"Yep. She also gives tours of the museum. She seems to know a lot more than anyone gives her credit for." I didn't bring up my previous conversation with her. I figured he didn't need to know. "It was the killer, wasn't it?" I asked, changing the subject. "That was who bashed me over the head."

He sighed. "I doubt that. Portia is locked up."

"Portia is not the killer," I snapped, barely refraining from adding "idiot" to the end of that sentence. Why he insisted on blaming her was beyond me. Okay, so there was the matter of the fingerprints, but still—that could totally be explained by any decent lawyer.

"I'm afraid all the evidence we have points to her. I know she's your friend, but I have to deal with facts here." He stood up, as if to leave, when his phone rang. "Battersea. Uh huh. Where? When? Be there in ten." He shoved his phone back into the holster on his belt. "I have to go. Something's...come up."

"Who's dead?" I asked.

"I never said anyone was dead."

"You're the lead detective in a homicide. It stands to reason."

He gave me a long look. I couldn't read his expression. He'd have made a great poker player. "A body was discovered down by the marina. Killed sometime last night."

"Who?"

"Annabelle Smead."

☐

Chapter 17

There was no way I was lying around the hospital while there was a mystery to solve. The minute Battersea was gone, I managed to hoist myself out of the bed, find my clothes, and get dressed. All without falling on my face. Kudos to me.

My head was throbbing so hard I couldn't see straight, and I didn't have my car anyway, so I called Cheryl. "I need you to rescue me." I explained what had happened and where I was. The abridged version, of course.

"Are you nuts?" she snapped. "You need to stay right in that hospital where they can watch you and keep you from doing anything stupid." She paused. "More stupid."

"If you don't come pick me up, I'll walk to the marina." It was an idle threat. I'd be more likely to pass out before I'd taken a dozen steps, but Cheryl didn't know that.

She sighed. "Fine. I'll be there in fifteen minutes. Do not go anywhere."

The last thing I wanted was for a nurse to catch me and force me back into one of those awful hospital gowns and into bed. I did not appreciate having my backside hanging in the wind. What I could use was coffee and lots of it. I collected my purse from the cupboard and poked my head out the door. There was a nurse at the end of the hall having a conversation with a doctor. They had their backs toward me, so I figured it was as good a time as any for a getaway.

I stepped into the hall, closing the door softly behind me, and walked calmly toward the exit like I had every right to be there. Or not there. Whatever. I pushed open one of the big double doors and exited the ward without anyone so much as glancing my way.

Once I'd escaped the ward, I found a map of the hospital on a wall near the elevators. There was a coffee shop on the ground floor. Perfect. I stepped into one of the open cars and pressed the button for the lobby.

My phone rang, and I dug it out of my purse. Lucas.

"Hello." I tried for cheerful and chipper, but it came out a bit flat.

"What are you doing in the hospital?"

"Let me guess," I said, leaning against the wall of the elevator as it slid toward the ground. "Cheryl."

"You got it in one."

The elevator pinged as it came to a stop. The bitter scent of burnt coffee grounds permeated the air as the doors slid open and I entered the lobby. I grimaced, but decided bad coffee was better than no coffee at this point. I was also in desperate need of a painkiller. "Listen, Lucas, I'm fine. It's no big deal. Honestly."

He sighed. "I'm surprised you didn't get arrested. Or dead."

"Don't be so melodramatic," I said, striding into the coffee shop. Well, more like staggering. I must have looked a fright.

The middle-aged woman behind the counter took my order with an air of boredom. I wondered if I would actually get the caramel latte I'd ordered. Unlikely.

"Melodramatic?" His tone was deadly calm. "I think that's a little rich, don't you?"

I sighed. "Okay, so investigating without backup probably wasn't my brightest idea."

"You think?" he said.

Pretty sure he was being sarcastic. I ignored it.

"But I'm fine. I really am. The doctor says I'm fine."

"According to Cheryl, the doctor wanted you in overnight."

"He was being overly cautious. I can't stay in the hospital. I've got stuff to do."

"Snooping, you mean."

"That. And writing." Not that I'd written anything in days.

He sighed. "I've got an appearance on the news tonight, but then I can be down there by ten."

"Don't be silly. You're leaving for Phoenix in a few days. You do not need to babysit me."

"You sure about that?" he said dryly.

The barista called my name. Or rather, she called out "Ebola," which was probably not the brightest thing to do in a hospital.

"I've got to go, Lucas. I appreciate you worrying about me, but I'm fine. Honest."

He grumbled a bit, but I'd convinced him. More or less. It was awfully sweet of him to worry, but I needed to focus on finding the killer. And getting rid of this headache.

I snagged my coffee from the counter and sat down at a table with a good view of the front door. Sure enough, my first sip told me there wasn't a spot of caramel or any other syrup in the thing. Rather than get into it with the barista, I dumped in a crapload of sugar and called it good. Then I rooted around in my bag for painkillers. There were still two pills left in the bottle, thank goodness. I made a mental note to restock as soon as possible. I was going to need them. Apparently, crime solving involved a lot of bodily damage.

The minute Cheryl entered, I waved her down. She stomped toward me with a worried frown on her face.

"What are you doing down here? I thought I told you not to move."

"Clearly I have a listening problem. Let's go." I all but dragged her from the hospital, still a little worried I'd be spotted and hauled back to bed.

"Are you sure you should be out of bed?" Cheryl asked as she put her car in gear and headed for the marina. She drove a rather boring import that was half a dozen years old. I kept telling her she should get a newer car, but she ignored me. "You don't look so good."

"Gee, thanks for your glowing report." To be honest, I didn't feel so good, but she didn't need to know that. "Seriously, Viola, you look a little peaky."

I raised an eyebrow which set my head to throbbing again. "Peaky?"

"It means—."

"I know what it means," I interrupted. "I just didn't expect to be insulted after narrowly escaping a plot to murder me."

She rolled her eyes. "Don't be so dramatic."

What was with people telling me I was dramatic lately? "Somebody bashed me over the head and stole The Louse's secret journal detailing his nefarious shenanigans. If you don't call that attempted murder, I don't know what you call it."

"I rest my case," she said.

I gritted my teeth, but that made my head hurt, so I gave up and stared morosely out the window. It was raining. Again. Spattering on the windshield in a haphazard manner. The sky was a swirl of gloomy, gray clouds edged in black. We were in for a storm. Hopefully the police could gather enough evidence from the murder scene before it all got washed away.

Cheryl pulled off the highway into a graveled parking lot off 36th Street. A large sign pointed the way to the piers. There were several other cars in the lot including three police vehicles and Mr. Voss's mortuary van. As I swung open the car door, I could hear the loud barking of the sea lions that gathered on the empty docks below to sunbathe. Not that there was any sun to bathe in, but they didn't seem to mind.

I didn't bother with an umbrella. For one thing, it was far too windy. For another, I didn't have one on my person. I ignored the raindrops splashing on my head. Maybe it would hide the bedhead disaster that was my hair. The cold certainly made the massive goose egg on the back of my head feel better.

"Are you sure about this?" Cheryl asked as she locked the car. "I don't think the police are going to be thrilled with you poking around their crime scene."

"Tough cookies. If the police insist on blaming poor Portia for everything, despite the obvious, I'm going to have my nose in their business 24/7." I pondered the lack of sleep that would result in such dedication. "Well, maybe 12/7," I amended.

Cheryl shook her head. "Well, I'm going with you to make sure you don't fall into the bay or get eaten by a sea lion."

"Sea lions don't eat people."

"They might if you collapse right in front of them. Might mistake you for a tasty fish and take a nibble."

"Seriously?"

She shrugged. "It could happen."

"No. No. It really couldn't."

She ignored me and tromped across the gravel toward the paved walkway leading down to the docks. I followed her, still exasperated.

Nearby, clusters of people gathered to watch the excitement down on the pier. The usual looky-loos, tourists, and locals, no doubt. I frowned. Was that Blaine Nixon?

Whomever it was saw me and dodged out of sight. I was pretty sure it was Blaine, but I hadn't gotten a good look. How interesting that he was at Annabelle's murder scene.

Down below, I could see the police clustered on one of the wooden docks. Crime scene tape was strewn everywhere, and Battersea was shouting orders as the rain picked up. Mr. Voss and his minion had already collected the body, and the assistant was trundling it up the walkway in a black body bag. I shuddered at the thought of Annabelle in there. Poor thing.

"Mr. Voss," I called, flagging him down. "Is she really dead?" I gave what I hoped was an appropriate look of concern.

He gave me a sorrowful look. "Poor Miss Smead." He shook his head morosely. "Just a young thing. And with a sick child. What is this world coming to?"

"She is dead then? Annabelle?"

"I'm afraid so, my dear." He heaved a sigh and folded his hands in front of him. "Gone too soon."

"What happened?"

He glanced around to ascertain that the three of us were more or less alone. His assistant had disappeared into the parking lot with Annabelle's body.

"I heard the doctor say 'blunt force trauma.' Of course, I could have told you that myself." He shuddered delicately. "Poor thing. Half her head was caved in."

My stomach turned at the visual. "So, she was killed the same way August Nixon was?" He nodded. "Bashed her right in the head with something heavy. No weapon though. Likely at the bottom of the bay by now." His whole face sagged as if the sorrow was too much to bear. "Well, I shall leave you ladies to it. Good day." He lifted his trilby before striding off after the assistant.

"Couldn't have been the same weapon, though. The police have that locked up," Cheryl pointed out with maddening logic.

"Of course not," I agreed. "But it could easily have been the same killer. Whoever murdered The Louse used a weapon of opportunity. The killer could have easily done the same with Annabelle. Poor thing."

"Out here? What on earth would they hit her with? A rope?"

"Fine. They could have brought something from the museum or something. Or maybe the body was moved." I stared walking toward the docks, determined to find out what I could.

"What do you think will happen to her little boy?" Cheryl asked. "Poor little mite. It's got to be terrible losing your mother so young."

"I'll ask Bat. He'll know."

She grimaced. "You just want to find out what else he knows."

I grinned. "Darn Skippy. Now," I rubbed my hands together, "let's get on with solving this thing, shall we?"

# # #

"Ms. Roberts, would you please stop annoying my people and get out of my crime scene. Why aren't you in the hospital?" Detective Battersea came roaring up the ramp, expression as stormy as the clouds overhead.

"I'm a fast healer."

He rubbed his temples with his fingers—a gesture he made often around me, I realized. "Ms. Roberts..."

"Viola." I was getting tired of his formality. Plus I figured it would throw him off a little. "I heard Annabelle was murdered the same way as Nixon. This means you'll have to let Portia go, right? She clearly didn't do it."

"One does not necessarily follow the other Ms. Ro—" I gave him a stern glare. "Viola. Just because the same method was used does not mean it was the same killer. Evidence still points to Portia Wren as August Nixon's killer. I'm sorry, but that's how these things work. With evidence."

I all but growled in annoyance. The man was getting on my last nerve. And my head hurt like the dickens. It did not put me in a good mood. "Portia is innocent."

"So you keep saying. I've yet to find proof of that, but there's a whole lot of proof she's guilty."

"Circumstantial," I said stubbornly.

"People have been convicted on less."

"Doesn't make it right."

"I agree."

That surprised me. As did Cheryl's sudden appearance at my side. I'd thought she'd stayed back.

"Hi, Bat," she said a little breathlessly."

"Cheryl." Battersea gave her a nod. Interesting. He seemed to have such a difficult time using my first name.

"What about Annabelle's little boy? What's going to happen to him?" Cheryl asked.

I felt a little guilty about not asking first. But I was worried about my friend. My friend who could go to prison for life if I didn't help her.

"Annabelle's mother is on her way up from Arizona. She'll be here in a few hours. Until then, he's staying with a neighbor."

"Oh, that's good. Annabelle's mom is a sweet woman. She went to school with my mom," Cheryl said.

I breathed a sigh of relief that the kid would be fine. Well, not fine. But at least cared for by someone who loved him. Now I could focus on Portia without feeling guilty. Although I did. What if Annabelle had been killed because of the information she gave me? Then it would be my fault she was dead.

"Do you know why Annabelle was murdered?" I asked the detective.

"I know as much as you know at the moment. Now if you'll excuse me, I need to get back to work." He turned and started toward the dock.

"These murders are connected," I called out to him over the bark of the sea lions. "I'll bet you anything."

He paused and turned back, his face expressionless. "Then find me proof."

As he continued his stride down the walkway, I stared after him, grim thoughts swirling in my mind. "You better believe I will. If it's the last thing I do."

☐

Chapter 18

"You know..." I started as Cheryl and I climbed back in the car.

Cheryl groaned. "I'm not sure I can handle this without a drink."

"Too bad. No drinking and driving. As I was saying, I bet we could find some answers at Annabelle's house."

"Maybe. But I'm sure the police have it under control." She started the car.

I snorted. "If by 'under control' you mean they're happy to pin The Louse's murder on Portia....no. We need to find out all we can before the police get there."

She banged her head against the steering wheel. "What if we get caught?"

"We'll cross that bridge when it starts burning."

"We don't know where she lives." She was desperate now.

"Ah ha! Leave that to me."

A quick call to our bunco friend, Agatha, and not only did we have the address of Annabelle's apartment, but the name and apartment number of her onsite landlady.

Annabelle lived in nearby Warrenton, across the bridge and down the highway from Astoria. Painted in whites and blues, the tidy units were perched on a stretch of land across from a small park. It would have been peaceful if not for the busy main road zipping between the apartments and the park.

We found the landlady's unit easily and rapped on the door. It swung open to reveal a plump, older woman, perhaps sixty or so, wearing a purple and orange housedress with her hair wrapped up in a matching turban and fluffy pink mules on her feet. It was so stereotypical, I wanted to laugh.

"Hello, Mrs. Forrest?"

"That's me." She peered at me through thick-lensed glasses that made her hazel eyes appear larger than they were. "Who are you?"

"My name is, uh, Viola....Smead. I'm Annabelle's cousin."

"Oh, my dear," she said, reaching out to squeeze my hand. It was supposed to be a sympathy squeeze, but she nearly broke my fingers in her enthusiasm. "I am so sorry to hear about Annabelle. Such a shock. I didn't know she had a cousin nearby." I was surprised she'd gotten the news so quickly. Then again, small town grapevines could beat the Internet any day of the week.

"We were on our way for a visit," Cheryl blurted, "when we got the news. So terrible."

Mrs. Forrest frowned as she gave Cheryl the once-over. "You're not a cousin, too, are you?" Doubt dripped heavily in her voice as if she'd never heard of a multi-racial family before.

"Oh, no," Cheryl chirped. "I'm Viola's best friend. But Annabelle was a sweetheart, wasn't she? The news was such a shock."

"Oh, it was." It was Cheryl's turn to receive the sympathy death grip from Mrs. Forrest. "Sorry, how can I help?"

"Well, as you probably know, Annabelle's mother is coming into town," I said.

"For Timmy. Yes. Poor little guy." Mrs. Forrest clucked in sympathy.

"Yes," I agreed. "I was wondering if you would let me into Annabelle's apartment to gather a few things for my aunt to take with her. We'll get the rest later, but there were some items she needed right away, and I told her I'd stop by. I don't think she can handle it, you know?" I gave Mrs. Forrest a conspiratorial nudge.

"I understand completely. I normally would insist on coming with you, but I've a party tonight and I need to get ready." She blinked as a thought struck her. "Is that terribly insensitive of me?"

We assured her it wasn't and, after several reassurances that we would be quick and return the keys promptly, she let us go and disappeared inside. Cheryl almost wilted with relief.

"I can't believe that worked," she whispered as we scurried down the stairs and across the parking lot to the building where Annabelle's apartment was.

"It only did because this is a small town and the police haven't arrived yet. We need to make this snappy."

She nodded in agreement as we stopped in front of Annabelle's first-floor apartment. The key was a little sticky, but we managed to get the door open and get inside without anyone noticing.

The place was neat as a pin. I pulled out two pairs of rubber gloves and handed one to Cheryl.

"Are you kidding me? You carry these things around with you?"

"I do now. Can't be muddying the waters by leaving our fingerprints lying around, can we? The last thing we need is to join Portia in jail."

"Good point."

I glanced around trying to figure out where Annabelle would hide something incriminating. "I'm guessing she would keep anything sensitive either in her computer or tucked away somewhere like her bedroom or the flour canister. You're better with computers, so why don't you check her laptop?" I pointed at the machine on the dining room table.

"Am I looking for anything specific?"

I shrugged. "Your guess is as good as mine, but I'm betting it'll have something to do with the museum."

Cheryl nodded and sat down, flipping open the laptop. The sound of tapping filled the room as she got lost inside the computer.

I made my way first to the bedroom. With a small child in the house, it seemed the most likely place to hide something important.

Annabelle's bedroom was surprisingly...purple. Purple walls, purple and pink Persian rug at the foot of a bed with a purple, ruffled bedspread. Everywhere I looked there was so much...purple. Now, I like purple, but it was a bit much.

Next to the purple bed was a nightstand that had probably had its heyday in the seventies. At some point it had been refurbished with a white, shabby-chic paint job and fancy, purple glass drawer pulls. On top it was a lamp (purple shade, naturally), an alarm clock/docking station (ordinary black), and an e-reader (with purple cover). There was also a glass with about an inch of water in the bottom, a bottle of painkillers, and lip balm in a round tin.

Inside the single drawer was all the detritus people usually kept by their beds: phone charger, random change, throat lozenges, hairpins, and a pack of tissues. I swung open the door beneath it to reveals stacks of books, mostly romances.

I had no more luck under the bed. She had one of those long, plastic tubs on wheels stuffed full of winter clothes. Other than that, the area was a breeding ground for dust bunnies. A quick look through her chest of drawers was no more fruitful.

The final hiding place was the closet. It had one of those double fan-folding slatted doors. I kind of liked the dramatic effect of whipping them open at the same time.

I stared in shock. Annabelle's closet was a hot mess. The rest of her place might be neat as a pin, but it looked like a tornado had ripped through the small space, clothes and shoes shoved willy-nilly in every available space until it looked as if they might explode out into the room in a blazing attempt to escape.

I grinned. This was it. If Annabelle had a dirty secret, it would be here.

I pawed through inexpensive dresses, faux-leather handbags, and boxes full of cheap jewelry. Nothing looked out of place. I gave a grunt of frustration and dove in, digging deeper all the way to the back of the shelves until I felt something cold and metallic. I carefully pulled it out, narrowly avoiding an avalanche.

I stared at the thing in horror. It was an antique bookend, and it was spattered in a reddish-brown substance.

"Oh, my word what is that?" Cheryl gasped. I glanced up to find her standing in the bedroom doorway, hand on her heart.

"I think it's blood."

Before either of us could say another word, the sound of police sirens echoed outside. A little too close for comfort.

Cheryl let out an expletive. "What now? Bat is going to be furious."

"Not if he doesn't know we've been here."

"And how are we going to manage that, Viola?" she snapped.

I glanced around. Annabelle's bedroom window faced the front, which meant we'd be easily spotted from the parking lot. We couldn't go back to the living room for the same reason.

I poked my head into the bathroom. A small window above the toilet led to the back of the building, totally out of sight. "We go out there," I said, pointing at the window.

"Are you kidding me?"

"Not even a little."

With a huff, Cheryl stomped into the bathroom, climbed up on the toilet, and slid the window open. A screen stood between us and freedom, and she gave it a good push. It went clattering to the ground.

"Hurry it up," I hissed. I could hear the police cars screech to a halt outside. Cheryl pulled herself up and wiggled through the window with ease. My turn.

I dumped the bookend on the bed where Bat would be sure to see it, then I jogged into the bathroom and climbed up on the toilet. It wasn't easy hoisting myself onto the window ledge. The frame cut into my belly and ribs rather painfully. I managed to wiggle my shoulders through, but then my hips got caught in the narrow window.

"Cheryl," I hissed. "Help."

She looked up at me. "What's wrong?"

"I'm stuck."

She sighed. "What do you want me to do about it?"

"Grab my hands and pull."

She did what I asked, but I didn't budge. My hips were firmly wedged in the window with my head poking outside and my backside in full view of anyone who walked in the bathroom. Maybe the police wouldn't notice. Maybe they'd walk right by the bathroom without looking...

"Well, well. What have we got here?" Bat's voice came through muffled behind me.

I closed my eyes and let out a string of words that would have had my mother reaching for the soap.

Shéa MacLeod

☐

Chapter 19

"I should arrest you." Detective Battersea was not amused. Not that I blamed him.

We were sitting in Annabelle's living room. Bat and one of his officers had managed to get me unstuck and dragged me back through the window. It had been embarrassing to say the least. Cheryl hadn't even made an attempt to get away and was sitting primly beside me on the couch with an "I told you so" expression on her face.

"Hey, the landlady let us in. Nothing illegal here," I said stubbornly.

Detective Battersea glanced heavenward as if angelic beings might flit down to save him from my shenanigans. Good luck with that. "You knew very well that we would want to inspect the victim's home."

"I knew no such thing." I crossed my arms and matched him glare for glare. Liar, liar! Whatever. He couldn't prove I had known and, therefore, couldn't arrest me. Probably.

After finding the bloody bookend in Annabelle's closet, I'd planned to call the police. It was crucial evidence in a murder investigation. No getting around that. Unfortunately, I hadn't counted on the police getting there before I could do so. Now we undoubtedly looked guilty instead of snoopy.

"Ms. Roberts—"

"Viola. Now listen, Detective. I admit that maybe I let my curiosity get the better of me." He let out a loud snort which I ignored. "But the fact of the matter is, the moment I found anything of importance, I was going to call you. Wasn't that nice of me?" I all but batted my eyelashes at him, trying to play the innocent. "You just got here first, and I panicked."

Detective Battersea turned to Cheryl. "That what happened?"

"Yes, sir," she chirped dutifully.

"What I should do is arrest you and throw away the key." He sighed heavily. "Fine. Both of you get out of here before I change my mind."

We got. Just as fast as our legs would take us. Cheryl, being taller and fitter, made it to the car and had the engine roaring before I was halfway across the parking lot.

"Geez," I huffed, practically jumping into the car as she peeled out of the lot. "Good way to make us look guilty."

"I don't care. I do not want to spend the night in the slammer."

"Yeah. Does anyone actually call it the slammer anymore?"

She shot me a death glare.

"Okay, fine. Maybe this wasn't my most brilliant idea," I admitted.

"Actually, it may have been." I raised an eyebrow. "Oh, really?"

"Right before you found that bloody bookend, I discovered something on Annabelle's laptop." She gave me a smug smile as she backed out of the parking space.

"Go on."

"I found a string of emails. I think she was blackmailing someone."

My eyes widened. "She was emailing the person she was blackmailing?"

"No. Not that. She was emailing a friend and made some comments about how she knew some things about a local murder."

"August Nixon!"

She nodded. "That's my guess. The first mention of it was after his death. Then she made comments about how her life was going to be better soon."

I mulled that over. "Sounds like blackmail to me. But no mention of who she was blackmailing?"

Cheryl shook her head. "Nope."

"Of course not. That would be too easy." I sighed and leaned back in the seat. Rain was still coming down, turning the world outside into a muted blur of color. "I'm willing to bet that whoever it was, it was August Nixon's killer, and he, or she, also murdered Annabelle."

"That's a sucker's bet." Cheryl took a hard left toward the bridge leading back to Astoria. "Now what?"

"Now I think you better slow down," I said, gripping the edge of my seat. She'd taken the turn a little too fast for my liking. And as we barreled toward the narrow bridge, I could suddenly see us careening out of control and plunging over the side into the Icey bay.

Cheryl shook her head. "Can't." Her voice was grim. "That jerk behind us is practically up my tailpipe."

I turned to glance behind us. Sure enough, a big, black SUV with tinted windows was so close behind us he was practically in Cheryl's trunk.

"Tap the breaks," I suggested. "That ought to get him to back off."

She did as I suggested. No luck. He seemed determined to drive over the top of us.

"Why doesn't he pass us?" Cheryl asked, voice tight.

I didn't answer because it was obvious. The two-lane bridge was heavily trafficked at this time of day. He had no room to pass even if it had been legal. Instead he was being a jerk face.

We both breathed a sigh of relief as we exited the bridge. The highway expanded into four lanes as it entered a roundabout. Cheryl took the inside lane, circling left toward Astoria. The SUV roared around to the right. Then, without signaling, it veered into our lane and smashed the front end of Cheryl's car with an ear-piercing shriek of metal on metal.

We jerked heavily in our seats, my headache roaring to life, as our car careened into the middle of the roundabout, jerking and bumping over shrubs and flowers until it came to a stop against the "Welcome to Astoria" sign. The SUV roared off, fishtailing as it went.

# # #

"Didn't you just get out of the hospital?" Detective Battersea eyed me as I sat in the back of the ambulance.

I'd insisted I didn't need medical attention. They'd ignored me. My head hurt too bad to argue.

I shrugged, wincing a little as the action jarred my head. "I like to live on the edge."

He snorted. "More like survive by the skin of your teeth. She okay?" he asked the EMTs.

The female EMT, who had been taking my pulse, nodded. "It's a miracle, but she's good. They both are."

"I can't believe this." Cheryl was stomping back and forth next to the ambulance, her face a thunderstorm. "That car was practically new, and now look at it."

It was messed up, for sure. The entire front end was crumpled beyond repair, and there was a huge scrape along the passenger's side. Other than a seatbelt bruise across her chest, Cheryl was fine. Grumpy, but fine.

"What happened?" Battersea poised his pen over his pad of paper. I glanced at Cheryl. She was still fuming, so I quickly and succinctly told the detective what had happened.

"You get the license plate?" he asked Cheryl.

"What?" She looked confused for a moment. Then her expression cleared. "Oh, no. It happened so fast I didn't have time to react, much less think. It was deliberate, I tell you. I'll bet you anything this was another attempt to kill Viola."

"You're exaggerating," I assured her. Actually, I didn't believe that for a moment, but she was working herself up into a tizzy.

"I'm not. Every time you get mixed up in a murder, you end up nearly dead yourself!" It came out as a wail.

"You've gotten mixed up in a homicide before?" Detective Battersea's eyebrow went way up.

I shifted uncomfortably. "In Florida. It was no big deal. I happened to be at a conference where someone got killed. That's all."

"No big deal!" Cheryl squawked. "Two people got murdered. Not one. Two. And someone tried to push you down the stairs. And then the killer—"

Son of a biscuit, that woman had a big mouth. "Yeah, yeah. But it was fine. We all survived." Except those who didn't.

Bat cleared his throat. "I'll put a BOLO out on the SUV, but without a plate, it's going to be difficult."

Because there were probably a thousand identical SUVs in the area.

"And if you do find it?" I asked.

"Let me worry about that. You need to keep your nose out of this investigation before someone cuts it off."

Before I could blast him with my opinion, Bat turned and walked off, shouting orders left and right. You had to admire a man who knew how to take charge of a situation. Even if I did want to strangle him.

"Lucas Salvatore," Cheryl said in a sing-song voice.

I blinked. "What?"

"You're dating Lucas Salvatore, remember? Stop drooling."

"I'm not drooling," I snapped. "I'm merely admiring. It's not like I'm dead."

Yet.

Chapter 20

Cheryl thought I should go home right away and get some rest. Personally, I needed something a little stronger than rest, so I convinced the police officer who was driving us home to drop us off at Sip instead. He was reluctant, but in the end I triumphed.

"Good grief, what happened to you two?" Nina asked as we straggled in. She was in her usual spot behind the bar, wearing a black and white geometric dress that hugged every luscious curve. She had her hair up in a messy bun and wore dangly sapphire earrings to match her necklace and cuff bracelet.

"Which time?" Cheryl asked morosely. "The time someone bashed Viola over the head? Or the time we got run off the road and nearly killed?"

"We did not nearly get killed," I snapped. "We just ran into the 'Welcome to Astoria' sign."

"What?" Nina sounded horrified. "The one in the roundabout?"

"The very same," I said. "We've had quite the exciting afternoon." I managed to haul myself up onto a barstool, although it was dodgy-going for a moment there. My head still throbbed to the beat of an invisible drummer, whose butt I was going to kick as soon as I could think straight. "I need something stronger than the usual."

"I've got port."

"That'll do." What I could really use was a blackberry bourbon on the rocks, but I'd have to go elsewhere for that, and there was something so comfortable and homey about Sip.

While Nina poured, we gave her the rundown. Midway through the tale my phone rang. It was Detective Battersea.

"What have you got for me?" I answered without preamble.

"Seriously?"

"Time's a wasting. Well?"

He sighed. "I got results back from the note you gave me. No fingerprints."

"I figured," I said with a sigh. "Anything else?"

"Unfortunately not. Standard paper. Standard ink. And block letters are impossible to match."

I sighed, rubbing my throbbing temple. "Who would do such a thing?"

"How about someone tired of you sticking your nose where it doesn't belong?" he said dryly.

"So you sent the note then?"

"Very funny." He did not sound amused. "We also found out who the WTF from the journal is. Or, rather, what."

"Really? What is it?"

"Company out of Dallas that acquires items for museums and collectors. Totally aboveboard. They had no idea the items they purchased from Nixon were stolen. They contacted me as soon as they heard about the murder. I had them checked out. They're in the clear. Do you remember anything else about the journal?"

I sighed. "Unfortunately, no."

"Well, it was worth a try." He paused for a moment. "You have to stop this nonsense, Viola. That's two attempts on your life so far. Next time they might succeed."

They could try, but I wasn't giving up. Not even a little. I hung up the phone, more determined than ever.

"What note?" Cheryl glared at me as she clutched her glass of merlot like a life preserver.

I told her about the note that had been left on my car and the results, or lack thereof, from the crime lab. "Obviously the killer left it," I said. "And he, or she, thinks we're getting close."

"I can't believe you didn't tell me about this," Cheryl said, her brown eyes narrowing. "Why wouldn't you tell me?"

"I didn't want you to worry."

She literally growled at me.

"Sorry," I said lamely, "but I didn't take it that seriously at the time."

"Well, I hope you're taking it seriously now."

"Believe me, I am."

"I don't understand why someone would try to run me off the road, though," she said in a sad tone. "It's not like I'm the one investigating anything."

"True," I admitted. "But you're helping me."

"But how did they know we were at Annabelle's?"

"I'm betting they followed us from the docks. The killer had to have been there, seen us together, and realized we were in your car. Then they followed us to Annabelle's."

"But who?" Nina asked. "Were any of the suspects there at the docks?"

My brow furrowed as I thought it over. There'd been a small group of people gathered to watch the police do their thing. Most of them had disappeared when the rain started, but a few die-hard souls had stuck around. One familiar face stuck out from the crowd.

"Blaine!"

Cheryl looked up from her glass. "Who?"

"Blaine Nixon. August's son. He was there. I saw him. I'll bet he saw us, too. He had to be the one who ran us off the road."

"Then you should call Bat," Cheryl said firmly.

"I will," I assured her. "But not until I confront Blaine. I want to hear what he has to say."

# # #

I wanted to march straight over to the Nixon house and confront Blaine, but the late hour combined with fortified wine and a head injury convinced me otherwise. I hit the hay the moment I got home and didn't move until the phone shrilled at eight the next morning.

I glanced at the caller ID. Agatha. I considered not answering, but she'd just call back. Besides, she might have some juicy gossip for me.

"Good morning, Agatha," I said, trying to sound perky and awake and likely failed miserably. She didn't seem to notice.

"Viola. Good. I caught you." As if she didn't know my only phone was a cell phone and therefore "catching" me was pretty much guaranteed. "I was talking to Mavis Buchannan. Her daughter works with the police. You'll never believe what they found in Annabelle Smead's apartment."

"Do tell." I tried to sound surprised and eager, although I knew very well what they found.

"It was a bookend. From the Flavel House. Annabelle stole it."

"How shocking!" I tried to sound dutifully horrified.

"Apparently she'd been stealing for a while. August Nixon, too, can you believe?"

"Did you hear anything else about it?"

"Funny you should ask. There was blood all over it. The bookend, I mean."

"Ew. That's not good."

"Not at all. And here's where it gets interesting." She paused for dramatic effect. "The blood was August Nixon's."

"That is interesting. You're sure?"

"Well, Mavis was. Got it straight from her daughter. And you know what that means."

I did. It meant that Annabelle Smead had been in August Nixon's office the night he died. And she'd stolen the bookend after he'd been murdered. Which meant that either Annabelle herself was the killer, or more likely, she'd known who the murderer was. And if I had to guess, it was the latter, and that was what got her killed.

☐

Chapter 21

The Nixon's large Victorian loomed against the gray sky, the greens and yellows brightening up the neighborhood with cheerful abandon. Who'd have thought it would be a house of mourning?

I climbed the stairs, my head throbbing slightly with each step. The lump on the back of my skull was smaller, but it still hurt like a son of a bee sting. I'd even iced it and everything.

Chimes rang from the other side of the door as I pressed the button for the doorbell. That set off a frenzy of yappy barking and tiny paws scrabbling against the wood, trying to get out and viciously rip out my throat.

"Tank, shut up." The male voice had to be Blaine's. The dog didn't listen. "Quiet, Tank, or I'll lock you in the damn basement."

Tank shut up. The door swung open to reveal a rumpled Blaine, who'd clearly just crawled out of bed, barely. He was still wearing pajama pants with his Iron Man t-shirt and his hair stuck out in several different directions. He squinted at me. "What?"

"Good morning to you, too," I chirped brightly. "I stopped by to see how you and your mother were doing." I gave him an innocent smile and held out the white bag I was carrying. "And I brought you pastries." To my mind, pastries were always an appropriate bribe.

"We're fine." Ignoring the pastry bag, he leaned down and scooped up what I could only assume was

Tank as the tiny dog made a break for freedom. I almost burst out laughing. Tank was a Chihuahua.

"That's good to hear." I held the pastry bag awkwardly in front of me, not sure what to do. "I thought maybe yesterday might have been a bit of a shock for you. You know, bringing up old memories."

"What do you mean?" His expression was a total blank.

"I saw you at the docks yesterday. Where Annabelle Smead was murdered."

"Oh, that." He shrugged. "Just passing by. Wondered what the fuss was about."

"Interesting. Because someone ran Cheryl's car off the road after they followed us from the docks. You wouldn't happen to know anything about that, would you?"

"Why on earth would I?"

"Well, you were there. You might have seen something. A dark-colored SUV with tinted windows?"

"Well, I didn't."

I gave him a long look. "Or maybe you're the one who was driving the SUV?"

His eyes widened. "You're nuts. Why would I do that?"

"Because you realized we were getting close to the truth."

He snorted. "And what truth would that be?"

"That you killed your father."

He stiffened, his face turning an angry red. "I think you better go now." He started to slam the door, but I stuck my foot in the gap. The door bounced off my shoe, and I tried not to wince. Believe me, it looked cool in movies, but in real life it hurt like a mother.

"Actually, I think we better talk; otherwise, I'm going to let the police know everything."

He went a little pale. "There's nothing to tell. I didn't kill my father. I have an alibi."

"Really? Because that whole thing about being out with the band is pretty weak. You could have slipped out at any time. No one would have noticed."

He looked downright ill. "Listen, I didn't want anyone to know before. But, um, I was with someone."

My eyes narrowed. "A female someone?"

"Er, yes."

"And not Portia." Obviously.

He swallowed. "No."

"Who?"

He sighed. "I really was out with the band. At the bar where they were playing, I ran into an old girlfriend. We talked. Had some drinks. One thing led to another." He shrugged.

"You cheated on Portia?" I didn't have to fake my outrage.

"I didn't mean to. It was an accident."

"What? You just tripped and fell into bed with another woman?"

"Well, not exactly—"

"Oh, shut up. You make me sick. I suggest you call Detective Battersea immediately and give him your real alibi."

"You're not going to tell Portia are you?"

I gave him an evil look. "What do you think?"

I stomped back down the porch steps, livid, calling Blaine all sorts of names in my head. It was a good thing he had refused the bag of pastries, because I was either going to ring his neck or eat an entire bear claw.

# # #

I sat in front of my laptop and glared at the screen while I munched on a cherry danish. Rolf and Scarlet still weren't cooperating. All I could think about was the murders and how I could help Portia.

I needed to go back through the alibis of all the players. Especially those who had wimpy ones, like Roger Collins and Mary Nixon. Not that I believed either of them did it, but I didn't know what else to do, and I couldn't sit around doing nothing. So far, despite mounting evidence of her innocence, Detective Battersea was still convinced Portia was guilty. I had to help her.

I closed my manuscript, opened up a blank document, and began taking notes. Roger Collins had claimed to be at a pot party, and the police had supposedly confirmed this. But was he actually there? Could he have slipped out while everyone else was dancing with fairies (or whatever happened at pot parties)?

Mary Nixon had claimed to be at the movies with friends. Was that the truth? She could have convinced her friends to lie for her while she went and koshed her husband over the head. Didn't they always say the most likely suspect was the spouse?

I needed to find out who Mary's friends were and question them. And then I needed to find out who was at that pot party. The police may have already questioned everyone, but in my experience, people will tell writers things they would never tell the police. Mostly because they all think they've got an interesting story to tell. Sometimes they're right.

I knew one person who might be able to help me with my inquiries. Agatha. She answered her phone immediately.

"What do you know about pot parties?" I asked without preamble. Most people are shocked to hear little old ladies know anything about pot. I was not. I happened to know Agatha was a hippie back in her day.

She chuckled. "Are you talking about that ridiculous club where everyone gets together and smokes each other's pot?"

"Apparently. Roger Collins claims he was at one the night August Nixon was murdered."

"Well, then you should talk to Jimmy Vargas down at the Green Apothecary. He's got his finger on everything pot-related in this town." She gave me Jimmy's name, number, and the address for his pot store. Er, marijuana dispensary.

"What about Mary Nixon?"

"Oh, she's not into pot."

"No, I mean, do you know who she hangs out with? Who her friends are?"

"Darla Manes and Lisa Cutty," Agatha said without hesitation. "Been thick as thieves since high school, those three."

The perfect friends to back up an alibi. The kind of friends who'd lie for you.

After I'd collected their details from Agatha, I thanked her profusely, promised to bring pineapple upside-down cake to the next bunco night, and hung up.

I knew Jimmy Vargas by reputation only, but I figured he'd be easy to find since he ran the local pot shop, The Green Apothecary. Yeah, I found the name amusing, too.

The pot shop was located right downtown in one of the more historical buildings. A green neon sign shaped like a cross shone brightly out front. Once pot had been made legal in Oregon, those type of places had sprung up practically overnight. There were three of them on Marine Drive alone.

The bell above the door jingled merrily as I pushed my way inside. A middle-aged man with a neatly trimmed goatee and little, round glasses stood behind a long, glass counter, labelling edibles with a price gun. He glanced up. "Can I help you?"

"Are you Jimmy Vargas?"

He grinned. "Sure, man."

"I'm Viola Roberts." I stuck out my hand, and he gave me a firm handshake. "Nice place you have here." It was cheerful with mellow-yellow walls and neatly stacked edibles in the glass case, like we were standing in a pastry shop.

"Thanks. I like it. What can I do you for, Viola?"

"You heard about the recent murders?"

He pulled thoughtfully on his lower lip. "You mean the one at the museum?"

"Yes. And the girl who was killed down at the docks."

"Huh. Yeah, I heard something about that. Sad stuff, man. Sad stuff."

"Very sad. I'm investigating the murders," I explained.

He squinted. "You a cop? You don't look like a cop."

"Er, no. More of a private thing."

"Cool. Never met a private eye before."

He still hadn't, but I figured it didn't hurt to let him keep thinking along those lines. "I was wondering if you could help me with something."

"Don't see how I could be any help, but I'll do what I can."

I leaned against the counter. "You know Roger Collins? Works up at the museum."

"Sure. Rog and I go way back. He's been coming to my pot parties for years. Even before it was all kosher, if you know what I mean." He winked.

"He said he was at one of those parties the night August Nixon was murdered up at Flavel House."

Jimmy frowned. "What day was that?"

"Last Thursday."

"Oh, yeah. Mariposa made the most epic pot cupcakes. Peanut butter cupcake with chocolate frosting. Totally brought edibles to a new level, man."

"Sounds delish."

"Bet I can get you the recipe," he offered.

"Maybe later." I couldn't imagine whipping up pot cupcakes in my kitchen. My drugs of choice were caffeine and alcohol. Both in moderation. "Do you remember if Roger was there that Thursday night?"

"Oh, sure. He was there."

Dagnabbit. I'd thought for sure I'd be able to break Roger Collins's alibi.

"I mean at least he was there when the party started at six. After that, things got a little fuzzy, know what I mean?" He waggled his eyebrows.

"Yep. I get it. So, you can't confirm he was there at, say, eight that evening."

"Nope. Don't remember much after about seven. Or six thirty. Or something."

"How far was the party from town?"

"'Bout a mile down the highway." He jerked his thumb behind him in what was apparently the direction of the party.

So Roger could have easily snuck out and killed Nixon. Then he could have driven back to the party, no one the wiser.

"Tell you who you can ask, though," Jimmy said. "Mariposa. That girl loves to bake, but she doesn't partake. Diet or some nonsense. She was probably the only sober one there. She'll for sure know if Rog left or not."

Jimmy gave me Mariposa's cell number and wished me luck. He offered me a product sample, which I politely refused.

Outside, I dialed Mariposa's number. The woman who answered had a pleasant voice and a cheerful disposition. After explaining who I was and what I needed, she eagerly supplied me with the information.

"Roger was here all night," she assured me.

"Are you absolutely sure?"

"Oh, yes. We had a deep, philosophical discussion about ancient religions. I remember it perfectly."

"Thanks," I said and hung up.

Well, there went one of my suspects. Roger Collins couldn't have killed August Nixon. I had only one suspect left. If I couldn't prove Mary killed her husband, Portia might just wind up in prison, after all.

☐

Shéa MacLeod

Chapter 22

Tracking down Mary Nixon's cronies wasn't nearly as easy as finding Jimmy Vargas. Neither of them would answer their cell phones or their front doors. Since I had no idea what they looked like, I couldn't cruise through town hoping I'd run into them. Despite Astoria being a small city of less than ten thousand, the odds were not in my favor.

Google to the rescue. A quick Internet search revealed not only Darla Manes's Facebook page (and, therefore, plenty of photos of both her and Lisa Cutty), but also that she owned an events company called The Mane Event. Yeah, punny. She appeared to run said company out of her house, which did me no good, but I also discovered that Lisa owned a beauty salon called A Cut Above. What was with these people and their clever names?

I also learned something else extremely interesting. Something I couldn't believe the cops hadn't figured out already. I definitely needed to talk to Lisa…and quick.

A Cut Above was mere blocks from Jimmy's marijuana dispensary, so I chose to walk instead of drive. Why waste gas? Plus the sun was out, finally, and I figured I'd take advantage of it.

The salon smelled of herbal shampoo and peroxide. The top-forty played over the stereo system, and women of various ages chatted away at a dull roar while sleek-looking stylists did weird things with aluminum foil.

"Do you have an appointment?" A girl with spiky, black hair eyed me from behind the front desk. She was wearing blue glitter eyeshadow. Hadn't that stuff gone out of vogue in the eighties?

"No. I'm here to see Lisa Cutty."

The girl frowned and chewed furiously at a wad of pink gum. "She's sorta in a meeting."

"That's fine. I'll wait."

The girl shrugged as if to say "suit yourself" and stabbed a finger in the general direction of a row of comfy chairs in relaxed neutral shades. In fact, the entire salon was beiges, browns, and creams. A bit rustic but with a slight industrial twist. Very chic.

"Want coffee? Tea? A mimosa?" She recited the list like she was reading off a teleprompter.

"No thanks. I'm fine."

She shrugged again and went back to snapping her gum. I was pretty sure she was playing some kind of game on her phone. Around me, activity continued unabated as women were cut, washed, dyed, dried, and generally spruced up. Which reminded me that it was past time to dye my own hair. I'd caught a few strands of silver peeping out from the chocolate locks just this morning. Frankly, I was far too young to be going gray. Age gracefully, my backside.

After about fifteen minutes, a woman finally appeared from the back room. She was bleach blond, fake-tanned, and sporting far too much gold jewelry. Her white shirt was pristine, which made me suspect voodoo. Seriously, every time I wore white, I ended up with spaghetti sauce or something down the front. She strode over to me with purpose and thrust out her hand.

"Lisa Cutty. You're here to see me?"

She had a firm grip and shook with vigor. "Viola Roberts. Yes. I'm helping with the Nixon murder investigation." I kept my voice low, figuring she wouldn't want a lot of gossip flying around.

"Oh, really?" She didn't bother to lower her own voice. "How interesting. Are you a private investigator?"

"Something like that."

"It's terrible, isn't it? How he was murdered like that. Not that he didn't deserve it, mind you—The Louse— but I hate seeing Mary so upset. What can I do?"

"According to Mary, she was with you and your mutual friend Darla Manes on the night August Nixon was murdered, watching a movie at the cinema."

She crossed her arms and gave me a toothy smile. "That's correct."

"Interesting. Then how do you explain this?" I showed her the screen of my smartphone.

Her face blanked. "I don't know what you mean."

"This is a picture of you and Darla at karaoke night."

"So? We go to karaoke a lot. It's fun. You should try it." She rubbed her chin. Was that a nervous twitch? Or did she have an itch? I was going with twitch.

"Except this post is time-stamped and dated. Not to mention geotagged, thanks to social media."

"Again, what of it?"

I gave her a hard look. "This proves that you and Darla weren't at the movies at all the night August died.

You were at karaoke. And Mary Nixon is nowhere to be seen."

# # #

"Listen, Detective, I'm telling you, Mary Nixon does not have an alibi. This photo proves she lied." I practically had to chase Bat down the hall as his stride picked up pace.

I'd tracked him down to the police station and showed him my evidence. The idiot still hadn't been convinced.

"That doesn't mean anything, Viola. So she lied about her alibi. That's bad, and I'll check into it, but it doesn't mean she killed her husband."

I rolled my eyes. "Oh, please. One of the most likely suspects just had her alibi busted to little bits. She lied. Doesn't that mean anything?"

"It means she lied. There are a lot of reasons she could have lied about her alibi."

"Yeah, like killing her husband."

"Give me a break. Portia's fingerprints were on the murder weapon. It doesn't get more cut-and-dried than that." He stopped in front of a row of file cabinets and yanked open a drawer. "Listen, I'm incredibly busy. I don't have time for this."

I practically screamed in frustration. Why was he being so pig-headed? "At least check it out. Find out what her real alibi is. If she even has one."

He sighed. "Of course I will. I told you I would. I do know how to do my job."

"What about the photo?"

"Email it to me along with the link. Let me look into this."

"Yeah, because you've done a stellar job so far," I muttered under my breath.

"Excuse me?" He raised an eyebrow.

"Nothing. Have a lovely day, Detective. I'll send that photo right away." And with that, I swanned out of the police station in high drama.

I was beyond annoyed. Bat wasn't taking this seriously. He was so convinced Portia was guilty he refused to listen to reason. Well, if he wouldn't confront Mary Nixon about her lies, I would.

Better yet...

I had an idea. I tapped out a text and looked it over:

I've found proof of who killed your husband. Meet me tonight. 8pm at the museum.

Perfect. I pressed "send," and the text winged its way to Mary Nixon. I imagined Mary reading the text, and I grinned to myself as I walked down the street to my car.

Time to catch a killer.

☐

Shéa MacLeod

Chapter 23

"Wait," I said, staring at the intruder. I was standing in the study right next to the fireplace where Portia had found August Nixon's body. "You're not Mary." It was definitely not a woman standing in the dark. A shiver went through me. The dark figure moved into the light, and I recognized him immediately. "Roger? What are you doing here?"

"You thought Mary killed August?" He snorted in derision. "She would never lower herself to such a thing."

I frowned. This wasn't what I'd expected. "So she got you to do it instead?" I didn't see how that was possible, since he had an alibi. One I'd confirmed myself.

"She had nothing to do with it." He sounded affronted. As if I'd majorly insulted him. Weird.

"Um, okay. But everything points to her."

He sighed. "I know. Lack of alibi. You were clever to discover that."

"That's me. Very clever." I gave a nervous laugh. Would you just shut up?

"It was nothing, really. All innocent and aboveboard. She was having a little Botox. Nothing extravagant, but she's a vain woman, as most of you are."

"Excuse me?"

He ignored my outrage. "She didn't want anyone to know about her little procedure. So silly. She got her friends to lie for her. Ridiculous. If she'd just told the truth, we could have avoided all of this nonsense."

"You killed August? But you have an alibi," I blurted. "I confirmed it with Mariposa. So did the police."

"Alibis. You know, they are so very easy to manufacture. It was easy enough to drop a little something in her drink. She literally never realized." He chuckled to himself.

"So, you slipped away, killed August, and slipped back. No one the wiser."

"Pretty much it, in a nutshell." He seemed proud, like he'd done something heroic.

"You killed August because he was going to frame you for the thefts."

"One of so many reasons," he said. "The man was a louse."

"So I've heard," I said dryly. "But what about Annabelle? Why did you kill her?"

He heaved a sigh. "I didn't want to. She was a sweet girl with a sick little boy, but what could I do once she started blackmailing me?"

"She saw you kill August."

"Apparently. She demanded money. It was to help her boy, of course, but I couldn't have it. I just couldn't."

My armpits were damp, and I could feel my heart thumping in my chest like a bass drum. "Why are you admitting this to me? Why aren't you telling this to the police?"

"Because I have no intention of turning myself in." As he spoke, he moved a little closer, and I realized he was gripping something in his right hand. It was an extremely sharp, extremely large knife. He'd apparently graduated from blunt objects. "You can't prove any of this. The police already put Portia away. They're not looking for anyone else."

I didn't bother pointing out that they were definitely looking for Annabelle's killer and Portia couldn't have done it. "You're just going to let her rot in prison for something you did?"

"I have no choice. Mary and I are about to start our lives together. I can't let anything get in the way of that."

"But she broke up with you. You said so yourself."

"What can I say? I lied. I needed to protect her. Silly woman thought being truthful was the way to go. I understand, of course, but she doesn't realize the lengths I would go to protect her."

"You mean August."

"He didn't just want to frame me, he wanted to destroy her, too. He learned about the affair, you see. Can you imagine what a man like that could do to a woman who'd betrayed him?"

I could. Everything up to and including murder. "I get it. I do. Still, you killed him in cold blood."

"It wasn't something I wanted to do, but I had no choice. And, like I said, you can blab all you want, but you can't prove it. I have an alibi, remember? And Portia's fingerprints are all over the murder weapon."

"How did you manage that, by the way?" I couldn't believe I'd gotten this far in the conversation, that he was actually answering me. Then again, he was crazy. Obviously crazy.

He laughed. "That was easy. I wiped it down. When she found the body, the idiot picked up the weapon. Stupid girl. Doesn't she watch TV?"

So that hadn't been part of his master plan. Just a stroke of luck. And either Portia hadn't remembered touching the weapon in her shock, or she'd lied because she hoped they wouldn't find her prints. I was betting on the former, since Portia was anything but stupid.

"What about the note." I should have shut my mouth and got out of there, but I had to know.

He blinked at me through the thick lenses of his glasses, totally confused. "Note? Oh, you mean the one I left for you on your car. Stroke of genius, though you were too stupid to heed my warning."

"So, it was you. But I didn't see you anywhere."

He actually giggled. "I drove by my house and saw you poking around, so I parked down the hill and walked back. It was just a warning. I didn't want to hurt anyone who didn't deserve it." He glared at me. "Unfortunately, you really can't take a hint. I'm sorry about bashing your head, by the way."

"Right. You didn't want to."

"Exactly. I needed to get that journal in case August doctored it in his attempt to frame me."

"I totally understand. I guess you're right. I can't prove anything, so I'll be going now." I tried to skirt around him, but he grabbed my arm in a bruising grip.

"What is that?" he snarled, looking down.

"What?" I tried to act innocent, but I was shaking as he snatched my phone from my hand.

"You recorded me?" he screamed, spittle flying everywhere. He threw my phone against the wall, smashing it to bits. "Now I have to kill you, you stupid girl."

"Wait!" But it was too late. He lifted the knife and swung it toward my heart. I barely managed to dodge out of the way, ripping my arm from his grip in the nick of time.

Without a backward glance, I ran like crazy for the study door. I could hear Roger breathing heavily behind me as he chased me. In the dark hall, I could barely make out anything. I tripped over an edge of carpet and went sprawling on my face. He was on me in a moment.

I rolled just in time to avoid a knife in the eyeball as the blade sliced down next to my head and buried itself in the floorboards. I kicked out, connecting solidly as he let out a grunt and staggered backward. I scrambled to my feet and was off running again.

Upstairs were several displays cordoned off by ropes. If I could get there, I could knock him down and tie him up. Then call the police. As plans went, it wasn't a great one, but it was all I had.

I took the stairs two at a time, my breath coming in short pants. Roger was hot on my heels, his feet thumping heavily on the steps.

I dashed into the room and snagged the nearest object. It was a large, porcelain vase. The idea of destroying it made me sick, but there was no other choice. The minute Roger rounded the corner, I bashed him over the head. The vase exploded, shooting shards across the room. He went down like a sack of potatoes. I kicked his knife away and untied a length of rope from across a nearby doorway.

Perching on top him, I yanked both of his arms behind him and tied them as tightly as I could. I was in the process of searching his pockets for a phone when the front door of the mansion flew open and shouts of "Astoria PD" echoed through the old house. Booted feet tromped up the steps, and a bright light pierced my vision.

"Viola?"

"Hey, Detective. Got your murderer all trussed up and ready to go. Also, I think you owe me an apology."

Chapter 24

"I can't believe it was Roger all along." Mrs. Nixon was sat daintily on a barstool while Nina poured her a large glass of Syrah. "He always seemed like such a gentleman."

"Still waters run deep," Nina said with a shake of her head. Light caught the rubies in her ears and sent sparks of red light dancing across the wall behind her.

"I'm not certain that the saying refers to murder, dear," Mrs. Nixon said gently.

"Probably not," Nina admitted.

"Your friend Portia will be released, won't she?" Mary turned to me, worry lurking behind her eyes.

"Oh, yes. Fortunately, Roger's confession was stored in my cloud, so busting my phone didn't do him any good. Detective Battersea assures me she'll appear before a judge first thing in the morning, the district attorney will drop the charges, and she'll be out straight after that."

"What a relief. I hate to think of that poor innocent girl in a place like that."

"What's going to happen to the museum, I wonder?" Cheryl asked, nursing her own glass of cab. "Both the directors are either dead or in jail."

"Don't worry about that," Nina assured her, leaning one hip against the bar. "The historical society will take care of it. Likely Portia will get a promotion."

Portia would be happy about that. She loved the museum. It would be her total dream job. And it might soothe the hurt over Blaine cheating on her. The Louse. Like father like son. She'd better dump that loser, or I was going to have to give her a talking to.

"I heard Lucas gave you a lecture," Nina said with a grin.

I glared at Cheryl. Blabbermouth. "Yeah, he was kind of pissed off I put myself in danger again. I guess he wanted me to wait for him to help. But I totally had everything under control."

"Sure," the other three women said in unison. "What? I did."

The bell above the door chimed, and in strode none other than Detective Battersea. Speak of the devil. Not that we had been. I just liked calling him the devil.

"Ladies," he said, his voice low like he was trying to be sexy or macho or something.

The ladies simpered back in an annoying manner. I rolled my eyes.

"I guess Viola shared the story of how we found the murderer," he said.

"We?" I all but shrieked as he settled himself on a barstool at the other end of the bar, out of reach. Smart man. "What 'we'?"

"Takes a village, Viola," he said with a smarmy smile. Oh, I could have punched him right in his smug face. "Can I buy you ladies a drink?"

"No thanks," I snapped. "We've got one."

"Speak for yourself, Viola," Cheryl said, shoving her glass toward Nina. "Fill her up."

I glared as my best friend played nice to my nemesis.

I never did get that apology.

☐

~~~

Enjoyed The Stiff in the Study? Then check out Viola's next adventure, The Body in the Bathtub, coming in fall of 2016.

Shéa MacLeod

A Note From Shéa MacLeod

Thank you for reading *The Stiff in the Study*. If you enjoyed this book, I'd appreciate it if you'd help others find it so they can enjoy it too.

Please return to the site where you purchased this book and leave a review to let other potential readers know what you liked or didn't like about The Stiff in the Study.

Book updates can be found at www.sheamacleod.com

Be sure to sign up for my mailing list so you don't miss out! https://www.subscribepage.com/cozymystery

You can follow Shéa MacLeod on Facebook https://www.facebook.com/shea.macleod or on Twitter under @Shea_MacLeod.

□

About Shéa MacLeod

Shéa MacLeod is the author of the bestselling historical cozy mystery series, *Lady Rample Mysteries*, as well as the *Viola Roberts Cozy Mysteries*. She resides in the leafy green hills outside Portland, Oregon where she indulges in her fondness for strong coffee, Ancient Aliens reruns, lemon curd, and dragons.

Shéa MacLeod

Other Mysteries by Shéa MacLeod

<u>Viola Roberts Cozy Mysteries</u>
The Corpse in the Cabana
The Stiff in the Study
The Poison in the Pudding
The Body in the Bathtub
The Venom in the Valentine
The Remains in the Rectory
The Death in the Drink

<u>Lady Rample Mysteries</u>
Lady Rample Steps Out
Lady Rample Spies a Clue
Lady Rample and the Silver Screen
Lady Rample Sits In
Lady Rample and the Ghost of Christmas Past
Lady Rample and Cupid's Kiss
Lady Rample and the Mysterious Mr. Singh

<u>Witchblood Mysteries</u>
<u>Coming Soon</u>

Made in the USA
Las Vegas, NV
09 March 2022

45309730R00116